Dear Reader,

Ballet has always been a very important part of my life, something I've shared with friends and practised just for myself. It's the first thing I want to do when I feel great, and something that always makes me feel better if I'm having a bad day. Learning new steps is fun, and practising a dance until you get it right can give you a big sense of achievement. And performing for an audience is the greatest feeling in the world!

I hope you'll enjoy reading about the dancing adventures that Tash and her friends have in Ballet Stars, and that the stories might inspire you to get up and dance yourself. I know, if you do, you'll have loads of fun.

Lots of love,

Jane Lawes

PS Tash and her friends get to dance en pointe because they have proper training and the right shoes. But you must never try to do that without a ballet teacher! Without training, you could get hurt.

For my friends, who make this big city feel like home

First published in 2015 by Usborne Publishing Ltd.,
Usborne House, 83-85 Saffron Hill, London EC1N 8RT, England.
www.usborne.com

Copyright © Jane Lawes, 2015

The right of Jane Lawes to be identified as the author
of this work has been asserted by her in accordance with the
Copyright, Designs and Patents Act, 1988.

Cover: illustration of dancers by Barbara Bongini;
pattern of flowers © Nataliia Kucherenko/Shutterstock

The name Usborne and the devices ♀ 👑 are Trade Marks of
Usborne Publishing Ltd.

This is a work of fiction. The characters, incidents, and dialogues are products of the
author's imagination and are not to be construed as real. Any resemblance to actual
events or persons, living or dead, is entirely coincidental.

A CIP catalogue record for this book is available from the British Library.

JF AMJJASOND/15   ISBN 9781409583547   03460/1

Printed in the UK.

Usborne
Ballet
Stars

Amazing
Arabesque

Jane Lawes

USBORNE

Chapter 1

Nearly there, nearly there, nearly there... The car turned another corner and Aurora House Ballet School was suddenly visible between the trees. The windows of the beautiful old mansion house glinted in the bright January sunshine and Tash felt excited butterflies pirouetting in her stomach. The Christmas holidays that she'd thought would stretch out for ever had flown by, and here she was, almost back at school for a new term.

Mum slowed down as they joined the queue of other cars passing through the big iron gates into the school grounds. As the tyres crunched at snail-speed over the gravel, Tash twisted round and looked out of the back window to see who was in the car behind them. She couldn't wait to see her best friends Dani and Anisha again. They'd had three weeks away from school for Christmas, and even though she'd been to Anisha's house to stay with her for one weekend, she hadn't seen Dani at all. Dani had wanted to come to Anisha's, but she lived too far away and almost all of her holiday seemed to be taken up with visiting relatives.

"I think ballet school must be the only type of school where everyone's *happy* to go back after Christmas!" Tash said with a grin at Mum, who laughed.

"Anyone would think you'd had a rubbish time over the holidays," joked Mum. "You've been packed and ready to come back for about three days."

"I had the *best* time," Tash replied earnestly.

Amazing Arabesque

After being away at school for a whole term, surrounded by people all the time and sharing a room with five other girls, it had been wonderful to be at home with just Mum and do all the things they loved to do together: watching films with mugs of hot chocolate, pretending to be TV chefs while they made dinner, walking along the river and making up funny life stories for all the ducks. She'd done lots of fun things with Maddy, her best friend from junior school, too, and she'd even visited her old ballet class at the church hall. But she'd missed her new school friends, and doing *barre* exercises in her bedroom just couldn't come close to the pure joy of really, truly *dancing*, the way she did in her classes at Aurora House.

Mum parked the car and Tash got out and stood for a moment looking up at the window of Coppélia dorm, where she'd be sleeping once again that night, and for all the nights to come until the Easter holidays. She smiled. It was good to be back.

* * *

"Tash!" cried five voices all at once when she appeared in the doorway of Coppélia with her suitcase. Mum was close behind with her other bag. Tash let go of her suitcase and heard it smack against the floor as it fell over, but she didn't care – she was already in the middle of a group hug with Dani and Anisha, hugging them back as hard as she could. Dani's parents were there too and they chatted to Mum while Tash looked around at her friends with a smile.

"I can't believe it's only three o'clock and I'm *still* the last one here," she said.

"I only beat you by about ten minutes," said Dani.

"Tash, come and look at these! I got them for Christmas," said Anisha. Tash went over to Anisha's bed and looked at her new iPod speakers. "Now we can listen to music in here."

"Cool!" said Tash. She hugged Laura, Toril and Donna, the other three girls she shared the dormitory with, and soon everyone was talking about what they'd got for Christmas and the fun things they'd done in the holidays. They chatted and laughed until eventually their parents started to talk about heading home.

"I should get going, too, Tashie," Mum said, calling her by the name she'd used when Tash was a little girl. Tash sighed quietly. In her excitement about being back at school, she'd almost forgotten that it meant saying goodbye to Mum again.

Outside in the car park, Mum pulled Tash close for a long, tight hug and Tash gripped Mum's coat, wishing she could make the hug go on for ever. She felt Mum kiss the top of her head and heard her say "I love you". Tash hugged her even harder and mumbled "I love you, too" into her coat.

"Have a good term, darling," said Mum, pulling back to look at her. "I'll see you at Easter."

Tash had said she wanted to stay at school over half-term because it had been so much fun last term, spending time with her friends and going on a special trip to see the City Ballet Company perform *The Sleeping Beauty*. She'd enjoyed it so much and had been so eager to go back to Aurora House after Christmas that she'd told Mum she didn't mind staying at school this time. But now that she was standing in the car park saying goodbye again, she wasn't so sure.

Dani and her older sister Helen were saying goodbye to their parents at the same time as Tash, and she caught up with them at the back door into the school building.

"At least we have ballet tomorrow morning," said Dani.

"True," said Tash, thinking of the big, bright studio they used for their two-hour ballet class each morning. She felt her sadness being pushed away by excitement – she couldn't wait to get back into the studio and start dancing!

"Trust me," said Helen, who was in her final year at Aurora House, "in a few days you'll both have forgotten all about home and parents. You'll have way more important things to think about."

"What do you mean?" asked Dani.

"Exams, remember," replied Helen. "All years have ballet exams at the end of the spring term. I think we have them this term because we have academic exams at the end of the summer term."

"I'd forgotten," said Tash. "All I've been thinking about is getting back to ballet classes and seeing you guys again."

She smiled at Dani, who grinned back and did a little skip of excitement.

"Are the exams usually difficult?" Tash asked Helen, feeling a tiny twinge of nerves at the thought.

"If you work hard this term you'll be fine," said Helen with a shrug.

"Easy for you to say," Dani muttered, rolling her eyes at Tash. "You can't put a foot wrong here. Literally."

Helen and Tash both laughed. Helen was one of the best dancers at the school, but Dani always exaggerated the difference between herself and

Although it sometimes took Dani a ... member sequences of steps, the truth was that she was a great dancer too. Tash hoped that, even though she often put herself down in a jokey way, Dani knew that she was as talented as the rest of their year. After all, only twelve girls and twelve boys had been given places in Year Seven at Aurora House, and every one of them had the potential to be a professional dancer. The next seven years at school would find out who was going to make it.

"I bet you'll have something more exciting to think about next week, too," continued Helen with a twinkling smile.

"What?" demanded Tash and Dani. They had stopped at the bottom of the stairs that led up to Coppélia.

"Pointe shoes," said Helen. She smiled widely at them and walked off before they could ask any more questions.

Dani and Tash looked at each other and identical

grins spread across their faces. They'd all received a letter from the school during the holidays telling them that they'd be starting pointe work this term and that their parents would need to pay for the shoes, but Tash had had no idea it would be so soon. Pointe shoes! They were *finally* going to dance on the tips of their toes the way ballerinas did! Helen was right, this *was* enough to put all thoughts of home immediately out of their minds. They raced up the stairs as fast as they could and burst into Coppélia to tell the others the news.

"Finally, finally!" sang Anisha, while they were sitting in the dining room that evening eating chicken with potatoes and vegetables. "I've been waiting to dance *en pointe* my whole life!"

"Me too," said Tash. "It's what you see when you think of ballerinas."

"Imagine *us* dancing *en pointe*," said Dani, and Tash pictured it – herself and her friends wearing beautiful, shiny pointe shoes with flat, square ends that would allow them to stand and dance right on the very tips of their toes.

"What are you talking about?" asked Lily-May, who was in the other Year Seven dorm.

"Pointe work," replied Tash.

"Helen thinks we'll be starting it next week!" said Dani.

Lily-May's face lit up with excitement, and she turned to the girl next to her to pass the rumour on. Before long, the whole of Year Seven was buzzing with the news.

"I wonder how much it will hurt," said Dani later that evening, stretching her legs out on her bed and pointing her bare toes.

Tash did a few slow rises onto the balls of her feet while brushing her teeth next to Anisha. She'd been so swept away by visions of herself dancing *en pointe* that she hadn't really thought about what it would actually feel like. Dani was right; it probably would hurt, especially at first. But something else began to worry Tash, too. Everyone knew that you had to have really strong feet and ankles to dance safely on your toes – that was why dancers didn't get to do it until they were eleven or twelve, sometimes even older. What if her injury just before Christmas meant that she wasn't able to do it?

"What if the foot I hurt last term isn't strong enough?" Tash said hesitantly.

She shuddered a bit, remembering the pain when she'd sprained her ankle, and how scared she'd been that she might never be able to dance again. Anisha looked at her with sympathy filling her dark-brown eyes. They all knew how devastated Tash had been when she'd had to miss out on performing at the Christmas fair.

"Maybe you should ask Miss Anderbel about it," Anisha suggested. "You must feel like it's been ages since you've been allowed to dance properly!"

"Three whole weeks," Tash groaned. "It's been torture! I did start practising *barre* exercises again in the last week of the holidays though, and Dr Stevens gave me some gentle foot exercises to do." Dr Stevens was the school doctor who'd treated Tash after her accident.

"That's good," Anisha replied with an encouraging smile.

"I had to do *something*," said Tash. "Not dancing for so long was driving me crazy!"

"Well, now we're back and we'll be dancing again first thing tomorrow morning. I can't wait! And I'm sure your foot will be fine," said Anisha.

"I hope so," said Tash. "I don't want to miss out on *anything* this term – especially something as exciting as pointe work!"

"Helen's feet sometimes bleed," Dani put in. "And she gets blisters. She showed me. It was gross."

The girls all pulled faces at each other and laughed. Tash smiled at Anisha in the mirror and Anisha grinned back. They were roughly the same height, both with long hair and brown eyes, although Anisha's hair was black while Tash's was brown. Sometimes Tash thought it was strange that they got on so well because they were so different – she was much quieter than Anisha, because she'd never had to shout over younger brothers to get heard, the way Anisha had to at home.

Dani was louder than Tash, too – and even though she had a habit of looking down at the floor while she danced, she was cheerful and confident. She never seemed to let anything upset her, and she was always the first to see the bright side of a problem. Tash was so happy that they were her best friends.

"I think the pain of pointe work will be worth it though," Dani continued cheerily, leaning against the bathroom doorway while she waited for Tash and Anisha to be finished. Tash nodded as she slipped out past Dani and got into bed. She sat under the duvet, hugging her knees to her chest with excitement. Anisha got into her own bed next to Tash's and an avalanche of her favourite pop music magazines slid to the floor. Tash couldn't help a giggle: they'd only been back for one evening and Anisha's little area of the room was already a total mess.

"Of course it will be worth it," Tash said. "Even if it hurts, just imagine standing *en pointe* for the first time. I bet it will feel like we're real ballet dancers."

"I bet it will feel like we're about to fall over," said Dani as she clambered into her bed on the other side of Tash's.

"Probably," laughed Tash. "But we'll practise and practise and then one day we'll be able to do *pirouettes* and balance in *arabesques* and it will feel like the most beautiful thing ever."

"I think you missed out a couple of hundred 'practise's," said Anisha.

"Let me dream," said Tash. "I know what I'm aiming for and, yeah, maybe it'll hurt at first and it'll be really difficult, but when – *if* – I'm a dancer at City Ballet I'll be glad that I practised so much."

"Don't practise *too* much!" Dani warned, with a look of alarm. "Remember what happened last time."

"I won't practise outside of classes any more," promised Tash. That was what had led to her accident before Christmas. "But I'm going to work as hard as I possibly can when I'm *in* class!"

Anisha smiled at her and snuggled down under her duvet. "You'll get there, Tash. I'm completely sure of that," she yawned.

"So will you," said Tash.

"Maybe," Anisha mumbled drowsily.

As exhaustion finally overcame her, Tash lay down and closed her eyes. And all she could see were pairs of pink satin pointe shoes lined up, ready for her to step into them and dance her way to becoming a ballerina at City Ballet.

Chapter 2

It was hard to get out of bed on Monday morning. After the comfort of being at home during the lazy Christmas holidays, waking up late and eating breakfast in pyjamas in front of the TV, it was tough to be woken up by the school bell again. But once she started getting dressed for her morning ballet class, Tash felt a buzz of excitement. She pulled on a pair of pink ballet tights and her navy-blue school leotard, and slipped her school tracksuit trousers and zip-up hoody on top to keep warm.

Everyone else was quiet and yawning as they put their hair up and sorted out their ballet shoes and school books. No one really came to life until they got down to the noisy dining room for breakfast, and then it was impossible not to get caught up in the enthusiasm and thrill of life at ballet school.

Tash and her friends found space at the end of one of the long wooden tables and chatted while they drank fruit juice and ate cereal.

"I hope we'll be working towards a performance again, like last term," said Anisha.

"We probably won't be," said Dani. "Not with the exams coming up."

Anisha looked glumly down at the last few cornflakes in her bowl. "I hate exams," she said.

"*Everyone* hates exams," said Tash.

"But at least we've got something to look forward to," said Dani. "Why don't we ask Miss

Anderbel when we'll be starting pointe work once we get to class?"

Tash paused with her last spoonful of cereal halfway to her mouth as excitement began to rush through her all over again. Then her spoon clattered back into the bowl and she and her friends were on their way to their ballet class.

The twelve Year Seven girls stood in the Hartley Studio, waiting for the first class of the term to begin. The big studio was named after Abigail Hartley, the school's founder. There were huge mirrors along two of the walls, with wooden *barres* attached to them, and windows just underneath the high ceiling that showed rectangles of pale grey sky. There was a piano at one end of the studio, which was used for rehearsals and for the senior students' classes, and a big music system set into one of the walls that played the music for the younger students.

"Welcome back, everyone," Miss Anderbel

said. "I hope you all had a good time over Christmas…but I hope you remembered to stretch and do a bit of practising as well!"

"I hardly did any," Anisha murmured to Tash with a grimace, and Tash grimaced back.

"This is an important term for you," said Miss Anderbel. "Every year, at the end of the spring term, all Aurora House students take a ballet exam. It's not an external exam, like you might have done at your ballet classes before you came here. You'll be assessed by me and your other dance teachers. But that doesn't make it any less of a test." She looked around the studio seriously, making sure they all understood how important the exam was. Tash caught Dani's eye in the mirror and saw that they had matching worried expressions on their faces.

"There won't be any choreography to learn," Miss Anderbel told them. "It will be like a normal ballet class, so you'll do exercises at the *barre* and then some in the centre – slow *adage* exercises, some *pirouettes*, small jumps and then *grand allegro*, big leaps across the room. It will focus completely on the basics, getting all the steps perfect, and not so much on performance – although, of course, you should always perform every exercise as if you're onstage. In fact, you *will* be on a stage – you'll be doing the exam on the stage in the school's little theatre where you performed at the Christmas fair."

Tash gasped and then her hand flew to her mouth to hide the sound. She'd missed out on the Christmas fair performance because of her injury. She was excited that she'd get a chance to dance on the school stage after all – even if an exam wouldn't be anywhere near as much fun as a Christmas performance.

"This will be our first chance to really assess the progress you've made at the school, and identify if there's anyone whose dancing we're concerned about. As you know, Aurora House students are expected to meet an extremely high standard." Tash nodded seriously, and as she looked around the studio, she saw that everyone else looked anxious too. "There's no need to look so worried yet!" said Miss Anderbel. "The end of term is a long way off and we've got a lot of work to do before then. Now, let's get to the *barre*, shall we?"

There was no time to ask about pointe shoes – everyone's mind was too full of the ballet exam to think about anything else. It sounded really scary!

Tash went to her usual place at the *barre*, between Anisha and Laura. Miss Anderbel started them off with a familiar *pliés* exercise that they'd done the term before, and it wasn't long before Tash was completely focused on dancing it properly and the feeling of her body stretching into the movements after the long break.

Miss Anderbel walked around the room correcting people here and there, as she always did – "Eyes up, Dani…very nice, Lily-May…move your arm *smoothly*, Toril…" – and the everydayness of the corrections and the exercise helped Tash to relax a little. But suddenly she felt a little twinge of pain in her ankle, and even though it didn't hurt a lot, fear shot through her and held her back a bit, stopping her from trying her absolute hardest.

She was so afraid of getting injured again that she didn't have the confidence to throw herself completely into dancing. *That* was completely unexpected. She'd been worried about the first ballet class causing pain in her ankle but she hadn't even thought about the fear of injury causing chaos in her mind. She didn't know what to do about it.

"Tash, don't push yourself too hard in this *frappés* exercise if your ankle doesn't feel up to it," Miss Anderbel told her, as if she could read her mind.

"But...the exam..." began Tash.

"...is a long time away," finished Miss Anderbel. "Just think about today."

Tash nodded and Miss Anderbel started the *frappés* music.

"How's your foot feeling?" Miss Anderbel asked a few moments later, stopping beside Tash while they did the fast, snappy exercise, striking the floor with one pointed foot and pulling it back quickly to rest against the other ankle.

"It's not too bad," Tash replied, even though it *was* hurting a bit.

"I'd like you to do some sessions with the school physiotherapist, just to be on the safe side," Miss Anderbel said. "You can start at lunchtime. I'll tell Miss Downing to expect you, so just go up to her room when you've had your lunch. It's next to Dr Stevens' medical room."

Tash nodded, disappointed that she'd have to miss out on having fun with her friends during break. But then she remembered that she'd be starting pointe work soon, and she knew it was important to make sure her foot was as strong as it could be. Giving up lunchtime was annoying, but giving up pointe work before she'd even started would be much worse.

"That sucks," Dani agreed, when Tash told her friends the news after class.

"Yeah," said Tash. "I know I need to build up strength again, but I wish I didn't have to miss lunchtime with you guys."

"Me too," said Anisha. "Hopefully it won't be every day."

"And don't worry," added Dani, "we'll keep you up to date on all the lunchtime gossip!"

Tash smiled at her friends. She hoped Anisha was right and that the lunchtime physio sessions would just be once or twice a week.

After lunch, Tash climbed the stairs, up past the empty dorms and the common room. She walked down the quiet corridor to the physio room.

"Hi," said Miss Downing, the school physiotherapist. "Tash, isn't it? Why don't you sit down? Now, Miss Anderbel said you sprained your ankle last term."

"It's better now," said Tash.

"All the same, you need to build your strength up again," said Miss Downing. "No good putting too much strain on it and getting hurt again."

"No," Tash agreed.

Miss Downing asked her to take her shoes and tights off and felt both her good and bad ankle, gently moving them around. Then she taught Tash some exercises that she could do to strengthen her foot – standing by the window and doing slow rises up through the feet in parallel and in first position, sitting on the floor and pointing and flexing her feet, and circling her ankles around.

As Tash repeated the exercises, she stared out of the window at the school field, where she could see Dani and Anisha and some of the others chasing each other, running and laughing and having fun. They didn't even look up and see her in the window, and she felt very far away.

"That's all for now," Miss Downing said at last. "I'd like you to come and see me every lunchtime for the next few weeks, just until your foot is back to full strength again."

Tash felt her face fall and she tried not to look too upset in front of Miss Downing. But inside she felt like crying. The thought of missing out on lunchtime with her friends *every day* was horrible. Her first day back at ballet school wasn't turning out to be as much fun as she'd hoped.

Luckily, it wasn't over yet, and the afternoon dance class turned it around completely.

Every day at Aurora House, as well as school lessons, they had two hours of ballet in the morning and two hours of another type of dancing in the afternoon – sometimes contemporary, sometimes character dance, sometimes *pas de deux*, which was where they learned to dance with partners. But today, Miss Carter, who usually taught them contemporary ballet on Monday afternoons, wasn't there, and Miss Anderbel was waiting for them in the studio again.

"Miss Carter isn't well, so I'm taking your afternoon class," she said. "We'll be doing another ballet class instead of contemporary. *And* I've got some surprise visitors for you."

At that moment, the door opened, and in walked four graceful young women dressed in casual dance clothes and wearing soft ballet shoes. But even if they hadn't been dressed for ballet, Tash would have known instantly that they were dancers because of the way they walked with their heads high, their backs straight and their arms held elegantly at their sides. They stood by Miss Anderbel at the front of the room.

"This is Ruth, Christine, Maria and Aniko." The teacher indicated them each as she said their names. "They're all soloists at City Ballet and they've come to help me teach your class today."

Tash nudged Anisha. "Maria was the Lilac

Fairy when we saw *Sleeping Beauty* last term!" she whispered.

"This is so cool!" Anisha whispered back.

"But first, I thought it might inspire you all to hear what it's like to be a professional ballerina," said Miss Anderbel. "So for one day only, sitting down on the floor of the studio is allowed!"

The class laughed as they settled themselves on the floor to listen to the dancers.

"Being a dancer with City Ballet is a dream come true," began Maria. "We're here to tell you all about it."

"I went to Aurora House, just like you," said Christine. "Maybe one day some of you will be back here, telling a group of students how you made your own dancing dreams come true."

Tash wanted them to talk for ever. Every word she heard made her more and more determined that she would have the same wonderful job one day.

"It's very tiring," said Maria. "We start dancing

at ten in the morning and if we have a performance we don't stop until about ten at night."

"But it's worth it," said Ruth. "We get to do the thing that we love most in the world all day long."

"Definitely worth it," agreed Christine, and the eager Year Sevens all nodded. "You have to be *sure* that it's the life you want," continued Christine. "And obviously there are days when you feel bad and your feet hurt…but if it really, truly *is* the life you want, then that won't matter. Because as soon as you get out on the stage with the music and the steps it's just…where you're *meant* to be."

Tash thought it sounded worth it, too, and she felt guilty that she'd wanted to go outside and play with her friends instead of going to physio.

"It's hard when you're at school," said Aniko. "Becoming a professional dancer seems so far away and sometimes it feels like all you do is classes and exams and schoolwork. When you first start pointe work it's really difficult, and it hardly even feels like real dancing because you just work on the basics over and over again. You have to be very dedicated."

Maria nodded. "If it all starts to get you down, keep your eyes on the prize," she said. "Stick on the DVD of your favourite ballet and remember what you're working for."

"Miss Anderbel, when are we starting pointe work?" Anisha blurted out.

Miss Anderbel laughed. "I might have known you'd be the first to ask, Anisha," she said. "You'll all be fitted for pointe shoes next week."

"Yesss," hissed around the room from almost everyone. Tash grinned at Anisha with delight and Dani clapped her hands together excitedly.

"Now has anyone got any questions for the *dancers*, instead of questions for me?" Miss Anderbel asked, quietening their thrilled voices.

"What was your favourite thing about being at ballet school?" asked Donna.

"The friends I made there," Ruth answered immediately, and the others all agreed. "I still dance with some of them at City Ballet. Christine and I started at Aurora House in Year Seven together! Some of our friends got jobs dancing in other countries, and we keep in touch with them still. When you're living together and dancing together, you become friends for life."

"You become family," said Aniko.

Tash shared a smile with Dani and Anisha. She already knew that was true.

When they'd finished talking, Miss Anderbel asked the City Ballet dancers to demonstrate the exercises that the class were going to do. Tash watched the dancers closely, fascinated and desperate to pick up even the tiniest crumb of help from them. They had the life she was longing for, and she wanted to learn everything they could teach her. There were hundreds of girls and boys taking ballet classes up and down the country – how many of them got the chance to learn from the best like this?

Then the students went to the *barre* to dance

the exercises themselves. Tash, Dani and Anisha bounced around on the balls of their feet while they were waiting to get started.

"I'm nervous!" squeaked Dani. "The dancers were so amazing when they did these exercises. I'll never be able to dance as well as that."

"You'll be fine," Tash said. But, although she was excited, she was nervous too: after a morning ballet class, all of their academic lessons and physio at lunchtime, she was getting tired. She really hoped that she'd be able to dance well and show the professional dancers what she could do. She tried to calm herself down by facing the mirror and watching herself do a few *demi-pliés*, but her insides still felt as if they were jumping around.

Tash soon settled into the familiar steps of the exercises though, and she could see that further along the *barre*, Dani was doing well too. As they turned around to face the other way and do their *developpés* exercise on the other leg, Anisha grimaced at her.

Amazing Arabesque

"We already did this exercise this morning," she grumbled. "Isn't once a day enough?"

Tash smiled at Anisha, thinking that her friend must be as tired as she was.

Towards the end of the *barre* exercises, while the professionals walked around with Miss Anderbel watching the Year Sevens, Maria stopped by Tash. Tash kept her eyes facing forward, but she could feel Maria standing there and it made her nervous all over again. She gripped the *barre* tightly and tried not to think about the fact that a real ballerina was watching her dance. She was desperate for Maria to think she was good, and it was suddenly really difficult to focus on what she was doing.

"Don't let your upper body move in your *grands battements*," Maria said quietly. Tash looked at her and nodded, breathless and shy. She really concentrated on keeping her body still while she swished her foot forwards and kicked her leg out straight in front of her.

"Perfect!" exclaimed the dancer. Tash glowed with pleasure. She smiled and whispered "thanks" while she carried on with the exercise.

From: twirling_tash
To: marianne.marks
Subject: Hi Mum

Hi Mum!
I have so much to tell you! Some dancers from City Ballet came to our class today and they watched us dance and told us all about being professional ballerinas. It was sooooo amazing. One of them watched me doing one of the barre exercises and she said I was doing it perfectly! How cool is that?! I have to see the school physiotherapist at lunchtimes because of my injured ankle. I wish I didn't have to, because it makes me miss out on having fun with Dani and Anisha. But there's good news, too. Miss Anderbel said we're going to start pointe work next week.

I can't wait! But what if my foot isn't strong enough? I keep worrying, but I don't want to go on about it with my friends – everyone's so excited about getting pointe shoes and I don't want to ruin it for them.

How are you? I hope you're having a nice week.

I miss you.

Love Tash xxxx

Tash had only meant to tell Mum about the fun things, like the visit from the City Ballet dancers, but then she started writing about pointe shoes and all her worries came rushing out through her fingers onto the computer screen. It made her feel a bit better to tell Mum how she felt about having to do physio, and she kept refreshing her email inbox until a reply appeared:

From: marianne.marks
To: twirling_tash

Ballet Stars

Subject: RE: Hi Mum!

Hi Tash darling!

The visit from the City Ballet dancers sounds wonderful, what a lovely opportunity.

I'm sorry your ankle is still troubling you. Have you spoken to your teachers or the physiotherapist about how worried you are about pointe work? I really think you should, I'm sure they can give you good advice.

Dani and Anisha will support you too, you know – they're your best friends, after all!

I love you so much and I miss you too.

Love Mum xxxx

Mum was right, Tash realized when she woke up the next morning. Talking to Miss Anderbel was the best thing to do and she decided to do it as soon as she could.

"Why are you rushing so much?" grumbled Anisha, when they were on their way to the studio after breakfast. "We've still got ten minutes until class starts."

"I want to talk to Miss Anderbel about something," Tash replied.

"What?" asked Dani.

"Nothing," Tash said hesitantly. "Just physio and stuff." She didn't want to make a big deal out of it. It would seem odd to her friends that she could be anything but excited about pointe shoes.

When they got to the studio, Tash went straight in to talk to her teacher while the others put on their ballet shoes in the changing room.

"Miss Anderbel," she began in a small voice. "Do you think…it's just that…I'm worried I won't be able to do pointe work…because of my foot."

Miss Anderbel listened as her worries came tumbling out. "I'm scared that it will hurt my foot and I'll get injured again!" said Tash.

"Tash, I'm glad you're taking this so seriously," she said. "But you have nothing to be afraid of. I've spoken to Miss Downing and she's told me that as long as you're careful and don't push yourself too hard, she thinks you'll be fine. You can start pointe work with the others and we'll see how it goes."

Tash grinned at her teacher and bounded back to the changing room feeling like a much happier person than the one who'd woken up in Coppélia that morning. Mum's advice had worked! Even from far away she knew exactly how to make everything better.

Chapter 3

Tash stood with her feet in first position and held onto the *barre*. She was wearing a pair of pointe shoes for the first time in her life and it felt weird and wonderful all at the same time. The ballet shop that supplied the school with shoes, leotards, tights and all kinds of ballet accessories had sent a team of people to fit the Year Seven girls with their first pairs of pointe shoes. One of them kneeled on the floor by Tash's feet and looked at how the shoes were fitting.

"Okay, try rising up for me," she said.

Tash took a deep breath. Her fingers gripped the wooden *barre* in tingly anticipation. This was it. She was about to go *en pointe* and become a serious, grown-up ballet dancer. She rose up slowly. It was surprisingly difficult to rise up through *demi-pointe* because the soles of the shoes were very hard. She watched her feet in the shiny pink shoes as she moved up to stand on the tips of her toes.

"How does that feel?" asked the woman.

"Okay," said Tash, still gripping the *barre* for balance.

It wasn't very painful to stand *en pointe*, but it did feel pretty weird, like she was a wobbly baby deer taking its first steps. Maybe it was supposed to feel like that. She looked at herself in the mirror and couldn't help smiling. Even though it felt awkward and she had no idea if she was doing it right, her feet looked *awesome* – beautiful and strong and very, very ballerina-ish.

"Right, come down and we'll try some others," said the woman from the shop.

Tash sat on the floor of the studio to take the shoes off. They didn't come with ribbons sewn on, so she slipped them off quickly and handed them back to the woman in exchange for another pair that were a slightly different shape. Pointe shoes had always all looked the same to Tash, but now that she was trying them on, she could see that the different brands varied in shape and feel. The other thing that had surprised her was the "block" part at the end of the shoe – it wasn't a block at all! Her toes went right down to the end of the shoe, where the flat part that dancers stood on was made strong and hard by special glue. The woman had given her some "ouch pouches" to wear over her toes: squishy padded pockets that covered the front parts of her feet so that it wouldn't hurt quite so much.

While she tried rising onto her toes in the next pair of shoes, Tash sneaked a few quick glances at everyone else. Dani was next to her at the *barre* with another shoe fitter, clearly loving every second of standing *en pointe*. In the mirror Tash could see Lily-May, one of the best dancers in their class, on the other side of the room, already looking as if standing on her toes came naturally to her. Anisha had had her turn already and was kneeling in the middle of the studio with Toril and Laura.

When Tash and Dani were finished and had been given a pair of pointe shoes each, they ran over to join their friends in the middle of the room and sat for a while comparing their precious new satin shoes and gushing over what it would be like to dance in them.

"They're so beautiful!" said Dani.

"I can't wait to try them out," said Tash.

"Our feet are going to look so great when we dance in them," said Laura.

Anisha stood up and put hers on. She started messing around, tapping them on the floor to hear the *clop-clop* sound they made. She started to tap out a rhythm on the floor with the shoes, and soon she was doing a silly dance to go with it. They all giggled and Tash smiled at Anisha's cheeky grin.

"Anisha, stop that!" Miss Anderbel's voice cut sternly across the studio from where she was overseeing the rest of the fittings. Tash stopped smiling and looked sympathetically across at her friend. If only Anisha hadn't let herself get so carried away – now she was going to be in trouble!

"If you're going to ruin your shoes before you've even been taught to dance in them, I'll take them away from you," continued Miss Anderbel. Anisha stopped giggling immediately and took the shoes off.

"Sorry, Miss Anderbel," she mumbled.

Tash felt awful for her and she felt a bit guilty for encouraging Anisha to mess around and laughing along with the others. Tash really liked Miss Anderbel and she imagined that getting told off by her for being silly in a ballet class would feel completely horrible.

That evening, there was a corner of the Year Seven and Eight common room where the only sound was the occasional yelp when someone pricked their finger with their sewing needle. Everyone was concentrating on sewing the elastics and ribbons onto their new pointe shoes.

"This is so hard!" wailed Anisha.

"At least we don't have to darn the toe bit like dancers used to in the old days," said Laura.

Tash rubbed her thumb across the patch of rougher material that was stuck onto the flat toe part of the shoe for extra grip, silently agreeing with Laura.

"My needle keeps getting stuck in the side of the shoe," Tash said.

They'd all learned how to sew ribbons onto their soft ballet shoes last term, but attaching the ribbons and elastic to the pointe shoes was much more difficult. It took a long, long time, but to Tash it felt like walking through another door on the way to becoming a professional dancer.

"Imagine how many ribbons we'll have sewed onto shoes by the time we leave school," said Dani.

Tash grinned, but Anisha looked at Dani in horror and then growled with frustration when the pale pink thread she was using slipped out of the needle yet again.

"I'm not sure it's worth it," she moaned.

"Of course it is," said Tash. "Here, let me try."

She held out her hand for Anisha's needle and thread. Anisha smiled gratefully when Tash managed to thread the needle, then she sighed, gritted her teeth and got on with her second shoe.

When Tash had finished sewing the ribbons and elastic onto her own shoes, she rolled up her jeans and put them on. She was disappointed that she hadn't actually got to dance in them yet. All they'd done with the shoe fitters was rise up and down. They'd be starting pointe work the next day, but Tash didn't think she could wait that long to try the shoes out.

"You shouldn't be wearing them outside the studio," Lily-May pointed out.

"I'm just making sure the ribbons are right," protested Tash. Breaking the school rules and using the studio by herself had led to her injury last term and she wasn't about to start doing anything dangerous again. She sat on the floor to tie the shiny pink ribbons, crossing them over and wrapping them around her ankles, then tying a knot at the side and tucking it under some of the ribbon to hide it. She stretched her legs out in front of her and pointed her feet as well as she could in the hard shoes. Then she stood up and placed her feet in fifth position. She rounded her arms in front of her and pointed one foot forwards, gazing down at it through the circle of her arms.

* * *

Amazing Arabesque

"They're so beautiful!" Tash told Mum on the phone later that evening. "And I spoke to Miss Anderbel like you suggested. She said I can start pointe work with the rest of the class!"

"So when will I get to see you dance in them?" asked Mum.

"Not for ages," sighed Tash.

She meant that it would take a long time to be good enough at dancing *en pointe* to actually perform anything, but as soon as she said the words, they reminded her that it would also be a really long time until Mum saw her do *anything*. She curled herself up small on her bed, alone in the dormitory.

"Is everything okay?" Mum asked.

"I miss you," said Tash.

"I miss you too, Tashie." There was silence for a moment. "Don't you need to be going to bed soon?"

"Can we stay on the phone for a bit longer?" Tash pleaded.

"Of course," said Mum. "Is something else worrying you?"

"Well...the exam at the end of term," admitted Tash. "It's so important – and I know it's a whole term away but it's already scary!"

When she'd done ballet exams at her old dance school, Mum had always been able to come and wait outside in the lobby of the church hall, so that she got a good-luck hug just before she went in, and a comforting cuddle as soon as she came out. She'd never done an exam before without Mum there. Who was going to calm her nerves about the Aurora House exams?

"Just keep doing your best in your classes and I'm sure you'll be fine," soothed Mum. "Will you have to dance in your pointe shoes in the exam?"

"I don't know," Tash replied in a small voice. She hadn't thought of that. Now she was even more worried!

"Whatever happens, I know you'll rise to

the challenge," said Mum, and Tash instantly felt a bit better.

The very next day she got the chance to find out what pointe work was really like. Tash had dreamed all her life of learning to balance and turn and glide across a stage in pointe shoes, but the first lesson wasn't like that at all. They started their class as normal in their soft canvas ballet shoes and they worked through the same *barre* exercises and centre dances they usually did. Tash *loved* ballet classes more than anything, but this one seemed to drag. She was impatient to put on her new shoes and it felt like Miss Anderbel would never get to that.

When she finally told the girls to put their pointe shoes on, Tash looked at the clock and saw that there were only fifteen minutes left of the lesson. How could they learn *anything* in that time? She could tell that her friends felt the same. She sat in a little circle with Dani and Anisha while they changed their shoes and tied the ribbons, all of them hurrying so that they'd get more time actually dancing. By the time everyone was ready and Miss Anderbel had checked everyone's feet to make sure they'd tied the ribbons correctly, there were only ten minutes left.

"Stand facing the *barre*, feet in parallel," said Miss Anderbel.

Tash did as she was told and looked at herself in the mirror. She could see the excitement in her dark eyes and feel it buzzing in her chest, and she bit her lip, waiting to dance. Finally.

But it didn't feel much like dancing. It felt more like boring, boring physio! All Miss Anderbel asked them to do was rise up onto the balls of their feet, just like they did in their soft ballet shoes, and then rise all the way up onto their toes. Up and down, up and down, slowly, four times. Then they did the same in first position. It felt good to stand *en pointe*, even though Tash found it uncomfortable to feel her whole weight pushing down onto the tips of her toes, but the shoes were still so stiff that it was weirdly difficult to bend her feet and rise up through *demi-pointe*. Tash was frustrated with herself until she looked at Dani in the mirror and saw exactly the same expression on her face. They couldn't help laughing and, looking around the studio, Tash realized that everyone was having the same trouble.

"I bet you weren't expecting that!" said Miss Anderbel. "Don't worry, your shoes will get a bit softer soon and then you'll find it easier." Tash stood ready at the *barre* again, but Miss Anderbel shook her head. "That's all for today. Go and take your shoes off."

A disappointed "Ohhh!" echoed around the room.

"I know it doesn't seem like very much right now," Miss Anderbel said to the class. "But trust me; it's best to build it up slowly. Even though *you* might love the idea of half an hour of pointe work today, I don't think your feet would. And besides, we have the end-of-term exam to prepare for."

"Will there be pointe work in the exam?" Tash asked.

"A couple of very short exercises, yes," said Miss Anderbel. "We'll start learning them soon."

Tash felt her stomach tightening with nerves and she shared an anxious look with Dani, who was standing beside her.

"In fact, before you go and get changed, I want to talk to you all about the exam," said Miss Anderbel. Everyone froze where they were at the stern tone in their teacher's voice. "I know I told you all not to look so worried in the first class of term, but I want to make sure that you all understand how important these exams are. I should warn you that if any of you don't pass the exam, we'll be asking you to repeat Year Seven."

Tash and Dani both gasped, and from the look on Anisha's face, they knew she was worried too. They all gathered their bottles of water and soft ballet shoes and were heading out into the changing room, desperate to talk about what Miss Anderbel had said, when the teacher called Tash back.

"Did that hurt your ankle?" she asked.

"No," said Tash. "Just my toes!"

"I think you should go and get checked by Miss Downing anyway, just to be sure. You can miss the beginning of your first lesson, just tell your teacher I sent you to physio."

Tash nodded but she felt her spirit sink further. She wanted to talk to her friends about their first pointe class and Miss Anderbel's warning. Now everyone would be talking about it all without her, and by the time she got to the maths classroom they'd have finished chatting and be getting on with their work. It was so unfair! She got changed quickly and slumped off to the physio room, feeling a little bit further away from her friends with every step.

Miss Downing told her to come back again at lunchtime, too, so it wasn't until that afternoon's science lesson that she had a proper chance to talk to Dani and Anisha. She couldn't wait to go over every detail of the ten minutes of pointe work with them. But they couldn't stop laughing about something funny they'd done at lunchtime. While they waited for everyone to get to the science lab and sit down, Dani and Anisha tried to explain it to Tash in between their fits of giggles, but she could only get a vague idea of what had happened.

"Sorry, Tash," said Dani. "We're not telling it well."

"I think you probably had to be there to find it funny," said Anisha.

"Quiet, please," said Mr Jones, who was ready to start the lesson.

The class settled down, and as Tash turned her attention to their teacher, she noticed Dani nudge Anisha and whisper something to her, and the two of them bent their heads over their books trying to stifle their giggles.

Amazing Arabesque

From: twirling_tash
To: marianne.marks
Subject: Pointe work

Hi Mum!

We had our first lesson in pointe shoes today! Well, it wasn't a whole lesson. Just fifteen minutes. But my feet hurt a bit afterwards. We learned to rise up onto our toes at the barre – I finally feel a bit like a real ballerina! I can't wait to learn more.

I had to go to physio afterwards, which was horrible because everyone else got to talk about the pointe class, and then I missed out on lunchtime as well. I wish stupid physio would hurry up and finish, it's horrible when everyone's talking about something I missed and I don't get the jokes. It's so unfair!

I really miss you.

Love Tash xxxx

Every day that week, they did ten minutes of

pointe work at the end of their morning ballet class, and even Tash was glad that it wasn't any more than that. Her toes hurt, although they were only doing the same boring rises again and again. She was desperate to get on to more interesting steps, but the truth was, she didn't think she would be able to do any of them.

When she held her pointe shoes in her hands, it was as if she was holding a whole world full of beautiful ballet dreams. As soon as she put them on her feet, the shoes became a stubborn, difficult reality. But Tash had always been realistic about ballet. She knew that it took years and years of hard work to do it well, and that was exactly what she had come to Aurora House for. The ten minutes of pointe work every morning were like the individual layers of net on a tutu – not much by themselves, but they'd build and build and build to make something spectacular. After all, ten minutes a day added up to fifty so far – almost an hour. She knew her feet must be getting stronger with every rise, especially because she was doing all the extra ones in her physio exercises, and the stronger she got, the sooner she'd be able to balance without holding on to the *barre*, and turn *pirouettes*, and balance in long, lovely *arabesques*.

She held on to that thought whenever she started to feel worried about the exam, scared about getting injured again or sad because she didn't get to see Dani and Anisha at lunchtimes any more. When she started to miss Mum, she pictured her feet in the pink satin shoes, and as lights out on Friday brought the week to an end, she drifted into sleep thinking about dancing, really and truly *dancing*, in her new shoes.

Chapter 4

School life continued in its usual pattern like a familiar sequence of ballet steps. The morning ballet classes were the happiest kind of hard work – hard because Miss Anderbel wanted to make sure they all did well in the exam, and happy because Tash really enjoyed the quest for perfect movement and still felt so lucky that she got to dance every day. At the end of every class, they practised pointe work. They were soon up to twenty minutes, and learned to do lots more simple steps at the *barre*.

Tash nervously held onto the *barre* and tried out a step they'd just learned for the exam, a *posé*: stepping up onto one foot *en pointe*, with the other leg held out behind in an *arabesque*. She'd tried it a few times already on her good foot, but she knew she needed to learn how to do it on the foot she'd injured. Stepping up onto just that foot was scary and as she did it, she was worried that her ankle wouldn't be strong enough. It didn't feel quite as stable as the other foot, but she didn't fall and she breathed a little sigh of relief.

Miss Anderbel had told them that in the exam they would have to step up into an *arabesque* at the *barre* and then let go, raising their arms to first *arabesque* position, with one arm pointing forwards and the other out to the side. If they were able to balance without the *barre* it would prove that they had learned to keep their weight in the right place when they were standing *en pointe* on only one foot.

Tash gripped the *barre* tightly for balance and then, when she felt steady, she tried to let go. She wobbled forward instantly and grabbed onto the *barre* again. She came down and tried again, this time holding on to the *barre* with only her fingertips so that she wasn't relying on it too much. That made it easier to slowly lift her fingers up so that she was balancing all by herself for half a second before falling forwards. It wasn't good enough for the exam – she'd have to be able to hold the balance for longer than that by the end of term. But it was a start. She looked at Anisha with a grin.

Anisha wasn't paying attention or even practising, she was chatting to Dani about the latest music videos they'd been watching the night before. Tash could see that Dani was trying to concentrate on the *arabesque* without seeming like she was ignoring Anisha. She was worried they'd both get in trouble and she was just trying to think of a way to get Anisha to leave Dani to practise when Miss Anderbel interrupted her thoughts.

"Let's try with the music," she said.

Tash stood ready to begin, her feet in fifth position, one hand gently placed on the *barre* and the other rounded and low by her side. Everyone else was ready, too. Everyone except Anisha. Even Dani was standing in the right position, while Anisha carried on talking. Miss Anderbel folded her arms and stared at Anisha with her eyebrows raised and an expression that said "I'm *waiting*".

"Is my class interrupting your chat?" Miss Anderbel asked.

Anisha stopped talking immediately and looked uncomfortable.

"You really need to start concentrating more, Anisha. These steps are going to be in your exam."

"Sorry," mumbled Anisha. She arranged her feet into fifth position and stood ready, just like everyone else. But when they turned around to repeat the exercise facing the other way, she rolled her eyes at Tash. Tash shot her a confused look back. After being told off, Tash had thought Anisha would be trying her hardest to please Miss Anderbel. Instead, when they started the exercise on the other leg, Tash noticed that Anisha was wobbling more than anyone else. She didn't seem to be trying very hard – what was the matter with her?

For the next few days, it seemed as if Anisha was trying to keep herself in Miss Anderbel's good books. But then on Wednesday she started to act strangely in ballet classes again. The music for an exercise doing *posé* turns diagonally across the room was happy and jolly, like something from a puppet show or a fairground. All of them had found it a little bit funny when they'd first heard it, but Tash was concentrating so hard on learning the exercises for the exam and getting the steps exactly right that she didn't think about making jokes or being silly. But Anisha made up a funny, jazz-hands, circus-style dance to the music and messed about in the corner of the studio while she waited for her turn.

Most of the class laughed, so Anisha kept going. She tried to get Tash and Dani to do the funny dance, too. Tash shook her head, moving forwards to stand in the starting position for the exercise. They were dancing across the studio in groups of three, and Anisha was *supposed* to be in Tash's group. Lily-May's group had nearly finished and Tash and Toril were ready to start, but it was obvious that Anisha wasn't paying attention. Luckily Miss Anderbel was too busy watching the people dancing to see. Tash looked anxiously around.

"Anisha!" she hissed.

But Anisha didn't hear. Tash sent a helpless look to Dani who was standing a little bit behind her. Tash didn't want Anisha to get in trouble, but if she called out to her, Miss Anderbel would hear and realize that Anisha was messing about.

At the last minute, Dani hopped in to take Anisha's place in the group. As she turned and turned across the room, Tash focused on "spotting" – fixing her eyes on a spot in the opposite corner and whipping her head around in each turn to find the same spot again so that she didn't get dizzy or lose balance – and she couldn't see what Anisha was doing. She reached the other side, finished the exercise neatly and immediately looked behind her to see what had happened. Anisha was ready to start dancing with the last group; her body, arms and legs looked like a ballet dancer's, but her head was still bopping comically in time with the music.

"Stand still, Anisha, other foot in front, Donna," said Miss Anderbel, and then counted them in, "…seven, eight, and…"

"You're extra-energetic today," Tash said to Anisha, when they were changing back into school uniform at the end of the class.

"What do you mean?" asked Anisha.

"You were so busy messing about that you forgot you were in my group for *posé* turns! It was lucky Dani took your place so Miss Anderbel didn't notice."

"I know, I was worried for a moment when I realized I should have been in your group! But I don't think it mattered. I did the exercise, didn't I?"

"Yes, but…" Tash looked up at her from the bench where she was sitting to tie the laces on her school shoes. "Miss Anderbel might get cross if she sees you being silly again."

"Don't take everything so seriously!" laughed Anisha. "I was just having a bit of fun."

Tash stood and picked up her bag from the bench. Dani was already waiting by the door, ready to go to maths. Tash didn't know what to say to Anisha. She was worried that her friend was going to get in trouble again, and she was also secretly hurt that Anisha thought she was being too serious. She knew that she could sometimes get a bit obsessed with ballet and with doing well in her classes. Did her friends think that she was boring?

"How's pointe work feeling now that you've been doing it for a couple of weeks?" Miss Downing asked, halfway through that lunchtime's physio session.

Tash was sitting on the floor, bending and flexing her feet and toes, and Miss Downing was watching her carefully.

"Fine," said Tash, hoping that if she said her feet didn't hurt at all, Miss Downing might say she didn't need physio any more and she could go outside and join her friends. She finished the exercise and stood up, knowing that a set of rises onto the balls of her feet was coming next.

"Really?" Miss Downing asked, raising her eyebrows.

"Well...it hurts a bit..." admitted Tash. "Sometimes I get scared about stepping onto pointe on the foot I injured. Especially when we have to step up into an *arabesque*."

Miss Downing nodded. "That's understandable," she said. "But a few more weeks of physio and you'll be back up to full strength again."

Tash's face fell and she turned her eyes towards the bit of the school field that she could see through the window. A few more *weeks*? It seemed like such a long time.

The next week it was Lily-May's birthday. Mr Kent, the Year-Seven form tutor, brought in a birthday cake with candles for her and they all sang "Happy Birthday" during afternoon form time. Lily-May handed slices of the cake around to everyone and Mr Kent let them all sit on the desks and chat for a while. It made Tash think about how her own birthday was coming up later this term, and for the first time she fully realized that she'd be spending it at school. She wouldn't get to have pancakes with lemon and sugar for breakfast with Mum; she wouldn't get to see Mum at all. Mum and Tash had gone to see a ballet on her birthday every year since she was six, but, like birthday pancakes, that was another tradition that was over now. Mum would probably send her a present and a card, but it wouldn't be the same. She couldn't send a birthday cuddle in the post.

"You okay, Tash?" Dani asked, licking icing off her fingers.

Tash forced a bright smile. "Sure," she said. "I'm just thinking how weird it'll be to wake up at school on my birthday."

"I'm so glad mine's in the summer," said Anisha.

"Mine's in the Easter holidays this year," said Dani. "But I think it would be fun to have it at school. We could have a midnight feast, like they do in boarding school stories!"

"Oooh!" gushed Anisha, her whole face brightening up. Tash realized that she hadn't seen Anisha look so excited for ages. "We should definitely do that, Tash. We could stay up all night and play truth or dare and make up dances and stuff like that."

"Yeah," Tash laughed. "And fall over our own feet from tiredness in ballet class the next day."

"Ugh," Anisha made a face. "Why is there *always* ballet-class-the-next-day to stop us having *fun*?"

"Because we're at ballet school, idiot!" laughed Dani.

"Ballet class *is* having fun," said Tash. She looked worriedly at Anisha. "Isn't it?"

"Yeah, yeah, I know," said Anisha. "I'm just joking."

"Are you okay?" Tash asked. It wasn't like Anisha to be so gloomy, and Tash was really starting to wonder what was going on in her friend's mind.

"Of course," Anisha replied. Her expression changed, as if she was talking to a teacher instead of a best friend. "Why wouldn't I be?"

"I don't know," faltered Tash. "You just seem—"

"I'm fine," Anisha said. "You've got chocolate icing on your chin."

Tash reached up her hand to rub it off, still worrying about Anisha. Whatever the problem was, Anisha obviously didn't want to talk about it, and Tash didn't want to upset her. Dani tried to go back to the midnight feast conversation they'd been having before, but Tash stayed quiet. She decided to keep an eye on her friend and see if she could work out what was wrong.

"We could do midnight games and dancing at a weekend, maybe?" Dani suggested.

"It probably wouldn't be that great in real life," said Anisha. "We're always so tired by the end of Friday, I doubt any of us could stay awake, let alone do any more dancing."

"Speaking of falling asleep," said Dani, hopping down off the desk. "Time to go to maths!" Tash and Anisha laughed and followed her to their lockers.

Amazing Arabesque

For the rest of the day, Tash watched Anisha for more signs that she was unhappy or worried about something, but she seemed completely fine all through school lessons, the afternoon character dance class and during dinner.

It wasn't until the next morning's ballet class that Tash saw her behaving strangely again. Anisha was staring up at the high windows while she moved her leg round and round in the circles of the *ronds de jambes* exercise they were doing. She looked as if she was hardly even trying! She'd seen Anisha messing about in between exercises or while she waited for her turn to dance, but now she wasn't even dancing properly. The exam was coming up and instead of trying to perfect everything she possibly could, Anisha looked more interested in the twigs tapping quietly against the window.

Tash remembered their conversation the day before, when she'd asked Anisha if she was okay and Anisha had brushed her off. Despite what Anisha had said then, Tash was sure something *was* wrong. She just wished Anisha would tell her what it was.

Chapter 5

Tash noticed Anisha's strange behaviour again the next day, and then the day after that. She couldn't watch Anisha very often during ballet classes, sometimes because she was in front of her or on the other side of the room, but mostly because Tash was working really hard for the exam and doing everything she could to get better at pointe work. That didn't leave much time for looking at what other people were doing. But whenever she did glance at Anisha, her friend was staring out of the window or whispering to whoever was next to her. Miss Anderbel didn't say anything, so Tash thought that she might be imagining things: maybe it was just a coincidence that the times when she looked at Anisha were also the moments when Anisha lost concentration. Maybe when Tash wasn't watching, Anisha was just as focused as everyone else. Tash really hoped that she was right. Ballet exam term was the worst time to lose focus!

"I'm so sick of this exercise, aren't you?" Anisha grumbled to Tash while they were waiting in the corner of the studio for their turn to do *grands jetés* diagonally across the floor.

"Not really," replied Tash, surprised that Anisha was. "I'm just trying to get better at it. I wish my legs would reach the splits in the air like the dancers at City Ballet!"

"Yeah, that would be amazing," Anisha agreed. "But practising it over and over again until we *can* do that is so *dull*!"

Amazing Arabesque

Tash frowned and her forehead wrinkled up while she tried to think of a way to answer Anisha without sounding like a teacher. Practising ballet never seemed dull to Tash and she couldn't understand why Anisha felt like that.

But there was no time to say anything; their group was up next. Tash, Anisha, Donna and Laura stepped forward and used the four counts of preparation music to *chassé* forward onto one leg and prepare their arms to third. Then they were off: *coupé-chassé-pas de bourrée, glissade, grand jeté*, leaping as high into the air as they could go with their legs aiming for the splits and their arms in first *arabesque, glissade, grand jeté, glissade, grand jeté*, higher than ever on the last one with arms thrown up gracefully to a rounded position above their heads as they jumped. The momentum sent them running into the corner of the studio as they came out of the exercise and Tash and Anisha pushed their hands flat against the wall to stop themselves, looking at each other and sharing a laugh.

"You have to admit that was fun," said Tash.

"It would be more fun if it was a rehearsal for a performance," said Anisha.

They turned to watch the next group, which included Dani and Toril, while they caught their breath. Anisha leaned against the wall of the studio, which was one of Miss Anderbel's pet hates. Tash was going to say something; she didn't want her friend to get into trouble. But then she was caught up in watching the others dance and marvelling at how high tiny Dani could jump. Way higher than anyone else in their class. She was amazing.

"Good, Dani!" cried Miss Anderbel, and then at the end of the exercise: "Better, Toril. You're working very hard this term. Right, everyone – left side!"

Anisha sighed loudly and pushed herself off the wall, trailing along behind Tash and the others to the corner they would start from to do the whole exercise again with their left legs leading.

Amazing Arabesque

* * *

Tash didn't know what to do about Anisha. She wanted to tell her that she was worried she'd fail the exam if she didn't work hard, but saying something like that would sound so mean, and even if she could find a nice way to say it, there was never a good chance. They were always in a ballet class or a school lesson or the common room with everyone else. Lunch would have been the best time but Tash was still stuck in the physio room every lunch break, wishing she was with her friends and wondering what they were doing. She wondered if Dani had noticed Anisha's problem too, but they were never alone without Anisha so she couldn't ask her, and anyway, she hated the idea of talking about Anisha behind her back. Anisha was one of her best friends and if she failed the exam and had to repeat Year Seven it would be awful. It would mean not being in the same class or dormitory any more. If she and Dani moved up to Year Eight and Anisha had to stay behind, it would be almost like being at a different school. Their little group would be split apart for ever.

On Friday afternoons they had *pas de deux* class with the boys in their year and because they worked in pairs, each girl dancing with a boy, it felt much more like rehearsing for a performance than morning ballet classes did. Mr Edwards, their teacher, always asked them to perform the short sequence they were working on at the end of the class, as well – usually split into three groups so that there were four pairs dancing at a time – and when it was Anisha's turn, Tash watched her closely.

She was brilliant. She and her partner Rob looked as if they'd worked harder than anyone in the two-hour class. Every step was absolutely perfect, and Anisha seemed like she was having the time of her life. She looked out at the audience of watching classmates with a confident smile, and it was as if she and Rob weren't thinking about any of the technical things at all, they were just dancing.

Tash was surprised, and she felt guilty for thinking that Anisha would be anything less than great. Maybe there wasn't a problem after all.

It definitely seemed that way at the weekend. Anisha was her usual self: fun and high-spirited, and doing impressions of all their teachers late into Friday night. Tash lay on her side in bed, watching Anisha and laughing hysterically. By the time they finally went to sleep, she felt much happier than she had for ages. She closed her eyes and felt her mind empty of worries. She'd done well in her ballet classes that day, Anisha had stopped acting strangely, and the late-night fun in the dorm had helped her forget what she might be missing out on at lunchtimes. Everything was starting to feel better.

When Tash woke up on Saturday morning, the room was bright even though the curtains were still closed. It was weird. Even on a sunny day, this much light didn't usually come in. She got out of bed and put her slippers on her cold feet. She shuffled across to the window to pull the curtain back and looked outside. The room got even brighter and Donna sat up.

"What is it? Where's that light coming from?" she asked sleepily.

"It's snow!" said Tash. "Wake up, everyone! The whole field is covered in snow."

Everyone else was just as excited, and as soon as they'd had breakfast, Tash and her friends bundled themselves into coats, scarves, gloves and woolly hats and tumbled out onto the bright white field. Almost the whole school was out there. The Sixth Formers and Year Elevens were building some pretty impressive forts using most of the snow on the main field, so Years Seven and Eight retreated round to the back of the school near the dance studios where the snow was untouched and perfect.

"We should be in teams and have an epic battle!" suggested Chris from Year Eight.

"Boys against girls!" shouted Sarah.

"No pushing anyone over," pleaded Lucy. "If any of us breaks an arm or an ankle or something we'll be in big trouble."

Everyone looked at each other seriously for a moment. They were all still dancers, after all. No one wanted their dreams ruined over a snowball fight.

"Ready…go!" shouted Jonah, and he pelted a snowball at Dani, who hurled one back and then ran away, followed by all the other girls. They regrouped in the little clump of apple trees where Dani, Tash and Anisha had spent every sunny lunchtime last term sitting and chatting.

"Some of us should stay here and make loads of snowballs," said Dani. "And the others can take them to hit the boys with."

"Good plan," said Lily-May. "Who's staying?" No one wanted to.

"Not me," said Anisha, crossing her arms across her chest as well as she could in her big puffy coat.

"I will," said Tash, seeing that no one else was going to volunteer.

"Me too," said Dani.

"We can switch over later," offered Anisha. Everyone made a few snowballs to start with, and then they ran off to catch the boys, leaving Tash and Dani alone.

They worked quietly for a moment, packing the snow tightly into rough snowballs.

"Hey, do you think Anisha's okay?" Dani asked at last, looking up and shaking her blonde hair out of her face.

"You've noticed too?" said Tash. "I thought maybe I was just being stupid."

"She's hardly even trying in ballet classes. I know she can't do the *arabesque* in pointe shoes at all," said Dani. "And the exam is getting closer."

"Should we say something, do you think?" asked Tash.

She felt so relieved that she could talk to Dani about her worries at last. Dani loved Anisha just as much as Tash did; they would both be devastated to lose her from their class, their dorm, their lives.

"Maybe," said Dani. "We might be able to help."

"But…what would we say?"

"Yeah, we can't really be like, 'Hey, we think you might fail the exam.' That sounds so mean. Even if we say it in a *worried* way."

"And if we say she should try harder then we'll sound like teachers or something," said Tash. "I already tried to talk to her about it and she just laughed it off. I thought…maybe…that it was just me being boring."

"No!" cried Dani. "I wanted to talk to her about it too but I didn't know how. I'm glad you tried, even if it didn't work. And you are definitely, *definitely* not boring. I don't think that and I'm sure Anisha doesn't either."

"Thanks, Dani. But I just don't get it! She was *so good* yesterday in *pas de deux*."

"And she seems totally fine today," said Dani.

"Maybe she was just having a bad morning," said Tash.

Dani raised her eyebrows. They both knew it hadn't just been one class that Anisha had slacked her way through. Just then, Toril and Laura ran up to them to grab some more snowballs, so they had to stop talking.

"Wow, you guys have made loads!" said Laura. "Want us to take over? You should go and help Anisha throw snow at Nick, it's hilarious."

Tash laughed and got up. She reached down for Dani's gloved hands and pulled her up, too. They gathered up some of the snowballs they'd made and jogged off to join Anisha and their other friends. Tash hoped a weekend having fun would get Anisha back to her old self again.

* * *

Amazing Arabesque

"Turn out, Anisha!" cried Miss Anderbel on Monday morning, sounding almost comically horrified.

They'd only just started class and already Anisha had been in trouble twice, once for trying to talk to Dani while Miss Anderbel was explaining what she wanted them to focus on in the *pliés* exercise, and now for not turning out properly. Tash exchanged a worried glance with Dani, but Anisha didn't seem as bothered as they were. She simply nodded at the teacher and turned out more.

As the class went on, Miss Anderbel's mood got worse and the list of Anisha's corrections grew and grew: ever-so-slightly bent knees when her legs should be straight, not paying enough attention and turning the wrong way in *adage*, messy double *pirouettes* when everyone knew she could do better, not jumping high enough, and not using her arms expressively. Their teacher was definitely in an everything-must-be-perfect mood, but even so, Tash had managed to get through with only two big corrections, and Dani with just the same one she had every lesson ("Eyes *up*, Dani, for goodness' sake!"). Tash felt awful for Anisha. She knew that if it had been her, she would have been miserable for the rest of the day. But Anisha simply shrugged the corrections off and sighed.

Anisha was chatting to Donna at the back of the studio while they waited for their turn to do *grands jetés* across the room when Miss Anderbel finally snapped.

"Anisha!" she shouted. "Every single time I turn around you're talking to someone. It's bad enough that you're not paying attention to your own dancing, but I won't have you distracting everyone else. If you're not here to work hard then you can get out of my class."

The whole room was silent and everyone stared at Anisha or at Miss Anderbel. Tash tried not to look at either of them. She didn't want to make Anisha feel even worse – out of the corner of her eye, Tash could see that she was biting her lip hard.

"I'm sorry," Anisha said quietly. "I won't do it again."

"Fine," said Miss Anderbel. "But I'm warning you now, if I have to talk to you like this again, I'll be calling your parents in for a meeting with Mr Watkins. You're an Aurora House student and we expect you to take our exams seriously."

"Yes, Miss Anderbel," Anisha whispered.

"Laura and Tash, you two were next, I think," Miss Anderbel said, restarting the class.

Tash tried to send a friendly look Anisha's way, but Anisha was looking down at her feet with her arms wrapped around her stomach as if she could protect herself from everyone's stares. There was nothing Tash could do.

Miss Downing had finally said that Tash only needed to do physio three days a week, so at last she had a lunchtime to spend with her friends.

She'd been so excited about having fun outside in the frosty grounds with them again, but that wasn't how it was turning out at all. They were sitting together in a corner of the common room because heavy rain was lashing against the windows and turning all the pretty snow to nasty, grey mush.

"Anisha, we're worried about you," said Dani.

Tash looked at Anisha anxiously. Would she just brush Dani off like she had when Tash tried to say the same thing? She thought that a common room full of Year Sevens and Eights might not be the best place to talk about it, but they'd started now and it was too late to take it back.

"Why?" asked Anisha.

"You must know why," said Tash gently.

"Because of class this morning? Don't worry, I'm okay. Just a bad day, you know?"

"Anisha…" began Tash.

"It's not just this morning, though, is it?" said Dani.

"What do you mean?" Anisha replied, sitting up straighter, her eyes darting back and forth between her two best friends.

"It seems like…in ballet classes lately…I don't know…you don't seem very *you*," Tash said awkwardly.

Anisha looked at her, hurt written all over her face. "Like when?"

Dani let out a short sigh. "Well there was that time you got told off for playing around in your pointe shoes…"

"And when you missed your place in *posé* turns," Tash reminded her.

Anisha crossed her arms and shook her head, as if those things didn't count.

"You tried to distract me or Laura loads of times in *barre* exercises last week," said Dani.

"I wasn't *trying to distract* you!" said Anisha, her voice rising in anger. "I was having a chat, that's what friends do."

"Not in ballet classes, though," said Tash. "And

I've seen you looking up at the windows a lot as well."

"You've been watching me?"

Tash started to shake her head. This was all coming out wrong. Couldn't Anisha see they were just worried?

"Why aren't you trying harder?" Dani asked directly. "We've got the exam at the end of term."

"What, you think I'm going to fail?" demanded Anisha.

"No…we didn't say that…" tried Tash, but Anisha was already on her feet.

"You're as bad as Miss Anderbel!" said Anisha. "Just leave me alone, I'm *fine*." She stalked out of the room, slamming the door behind her.

Chapter 6

Anisha refused to speak to them all afternoon, even though Tash and Dani kept trying to say sorry to her in between lessons. They had contemporary dance class at the end of the day and they were working in groups on their own choreography. Anisha, Tash and Dani were all in different groups, so there was no chance to talk then either. Tash kept looking across the studio at Anisha's group, hoping to catch her eye, but either

Anisha was purposely looking away from Tash, or she really was completely absorbed in the choreography. Tash was desperate to make up with her. Having Anisha still in her class but not being friends with her was just as bad as Anisha not being in her class at all. It might even be worse.

"Helloooo! Earth to Tash!" Lily-May was trying to get her attention, so Tash turned back to her own group with a sigh.

"What were the eight counts we made up right at the end of Thursday's class?" Rob asked.

Tash thought for a moment and then started to move, demonstrating the steps they'd come up with last week. Once they'd started dancing properly, she tried to focus. They'd have to perform for the rest of the class at the end of the lesson and she didn't want to let her group down. But it was so hard to think about anything except making things better with Anisha, and every few seconds, Tash's eyes drifted across the studio towards her.

After class, Tash and Dani changed back into

their school uniforms in silence. Anisha was getting changed on the other side of the room, as far away from them as she could get. Everyone had noticed that they'd fallen out – Tash knew it must be obvious because the three of them were usually so inseparable. She hated that everyone was looking at them and wondering what had happened, maybe even thinking that she and Dani had been deliberately nasty to Anisha. She kept her eyes down and looked at her feet as she wriggled them into her black school tights.

Whenever she and her old friend Maddy had fallen out, she'd been able to go home and tell Mum about it, and Mum had always been able to make her feel better. Sometimes she'd come up with the perfect thing to say to Maddy to make friends again; sometimes she'd help Tash see that it was only a little argument and everything would be okay. As soon as school had finished and supervised homework time was out of the way, Tash got out her laptop to email Mum.

Ballet Stars

From: twirling_tash
To: marianne.marks
Subject: Help!

Hi Mum

How are you?

Everything is awful here and I really need some help. Anisha's been getting distracted in ballet classes and being kind of silly. Dani and I tried to talk to her about it but it sounded all wrong when we said we were worried, and now Anisha won't speak to us! We were just trying to help, but now she hates us and I don't know what to do. Please help me think of a way to make it better.

I really, really miss you.

Love Tash xxxx

After she'd sent the email, she sat with her computer on her lap, refreshing the page over and over again. But Mum didn't reply. That was the problem with sending emails. She could pretend that she was talking to Mum, but Mum wasn't *actually* here. She missed Mum. And she missed Anisha too, even though it had only been half a day of not being friends.

Anisha ignored them all evening, and all through breakfast, ballet and school the next morning. Tash and Dani ate lunch together, missing Anisha so much that they hardly even spoke to each other, but they just kept glancing over at her sitting at another table with Lily-May and some of the other girls from their class.

"What are we going to do?" Tash asked in despair for the fifth time.

"We have to do *something*," Dani replied.

"I wish I knew how to make her see that we just love her and want her to stay in our class."

"Saying that will only make her madder," sighed Dani. "The *reason* she's angry is that we basically said she might fail the exam."

"But what if it's true?" cried Tash. "We can't just let her stop trying!"

"What if she doesn't care about dancing any more?" said Dani.

"She does care," Tash said firmly. "Don't you remember how she danced in the Christmas performance? And you've seen her in *pas de deux* and character class this term. She loves ballet as much as we do. I know she does."

"Then we have to remind her of that," said Dani.

Tash stabbed her fork at her pasta. "Yeah. When she starts speaking to us again," she muttered.

It was the same all through the next day, too. Anisha hung out with Laura and Toril, or with Lily-May and her friends. Every now and then, when Tash was trying to catch Anisha's eye and give her a friendly smile, Anisha did glance at her, but she always looked away again quickly before Tash could try to say sorry.

Amazing Arabesque

Tash was getting desperate. Mum had replied to her email and said that she should try to explain to Anisha what she was worried about. But Anisha wouldn't give her a chance, and Tash didn't know where to begin.

That evening, Tash decided she would try to talk to Mum on Skype. She needed to hear Mum say that everything was going to work out okay. But Laura and Toril were playing cards in Coppélia, the common room was as busy as usual, and Mr Kent was marking English essays in the form room. So Tash took her laptop to one of the music practice rooms. The music rooms were really meant for the students who played instruments to get in some practice after school, but they were often empty this late and Tash knew that she'd be able to get some privacy there. She'd managed not to cry over the fight with Anisha so far but she wasn't sure that she'd be able to stop the tears when she was telling Mum about it, and she didn't want anyone to see her so upset.

Ballet Stars

She walked past the tinkling sounds of pianos and the beautiful melody of a violin playing something from *Romeo and Juliet*, searching for an empty room she could hide out in while she talked to Mum. But they were all busy. The sound coming from the last room was so strange that Tash peeked in through the window.

No wonder it didn't sound like an instrument – it wasn't! Not unless feet counted as a musical instrument, anyway. What she saw was someone tap-dancing, and not just anyone. It was Anisha!

Tash watched her through the window for a moment. Anisha was hopping and tapping and turning and all the time her feet were making a fantastic rhythm. Tash couldn't help a smile spreading across her face as she watched. It was like seeing someone tap all their problems down into the floor and dance away from them, full of joy. She was so pleased to see Anisha being happy that she forgot about how horrible things had been. All she wanted was to go into the room and join in, tapping away in her slippers alongside her friend. Suddenly she couldn't stop herself, and she pushed the door open. Anisha stopped dancing immediately and turned to see who it was. Annoyance crossed her face when she saw Tash.

"What are you doing here?" she asked.

"I was going to Skype my mum," said Tash, nodding her head towards the laptop under her arm. She suddenly felt nervous – but she had to do *something*, she had to try to get her friend back. "You're amazing. At tap," she said.

"It's fun." Anisha shrugged. "More fun than ballet right now."

They were both silent. Tash was scared that talking about ballet now would make things worse again. This was the most Anisha had said to her in two days.

"Do you miss your tap classes?" Tash asked eventually.

"Loads," said Anisha, looking at Tash properly for the first time since she'd come in. "I used to do just as many tap classes as ballet classes. I started learning when I was four, just the same as ballet. Don't you miss it? You did tap before you came here, right?"

"I don't miss it, really," said Tash. "It was fun, but ballet was always what I loved the most. And now we get to do ballet every day – that's all I've ever wanted."

Anisha didn't say anything, but scuffed her feet through some angry-sounding tap steps.

"What's up?" asked Tash. "With ballet classes, I mean." She put her laptop down on top of the piano and sat on the stool. She hoped that Anisha wouldn't get mad at her for asking that again. "I thought you loved ballet."

"I do," said Anisha. She sighed and came over to stand next to Tash. She pressed her finger down on one of the piano keys and they both watched it sound a high note. "It's just the exam. It takes all the fun out of it."

"Yeah," Tash agreed. "But it can't be

performances all the time. Remember what the City Ballet dancers said? Eyes on the prize! We have to learn steps and work hard so that we're able to do them well when we *do* get to do performances."

"I know that," said Anisha. "But it feels like that's *all* we're doing. Just the same exercises again and again, every single day – it's driving me nuts. And even pointe work is like that. I thought it would be amazing to dance in pointe shoes but all we do are rises and *relevés*. It's boring!"

"I feel exactly the same thing about pointe work!" said Tash, agreeing with Anisha completely for the first time.

"But you look like you're enjoying every second of it," said Anisha. "How do you do that?"

"I'm thinking about where all the exercises are going to get me one day," replied Tash.

"The City Ballet Company?" guessed Anisha.

"I hope so," smiled Tash.

"It's easy for you," said Anisha. "You know exactly what you want. I'm not so sure any more."

Tash looked at her with wide eyes. "Do you want to leave Aurora House?" she asked.

"No," said Anisha. "I just wish we were having more *fun*."

"I'm sorry about the things Dani and I said," said Tash. "We really didn't mean to upset you."

Anisha nodded slowly. "Okay," she said. "I know you were just looking out for me. 'Cause you're my best friends."

Tash smiled and nodded. "Yeah," she said. "We are. No matter what."

"Even if we fight," Anisha replied. She grinned and Tash jumped up and hugged her.

They walked back towards the common room together. Now that things were okay between them, they both desperately wanted to see Dani and make things okay with her, too.

"I'm so sorry, Anisha!" Dani cried, jumping up and running over to them as soon as they came through the door. "I really never meant to hurt your feelings."

"I know," said Anisha. "I'm sorry I ignored you guys. I think I didn't want to admit you were right. It's so hard to keep focused when all we're doing is exam preparation. But I *really* don't want to fail and get left behind. I'm going to try much harder!"

"And…are we friends again?" asked Dani.

"Definitely," Anisha replied. Dani's face lit up with a bright smile and she grabbed Anisha for a big hug.

"Oh, you never got to talk to your mum," Anisha said to Tash later, as they were all getting ready for bed.

"Never mind, I can email her tomorrow," said Tash.

"You've been emailing her loads this term," said Anisha. "Is everything all right?"

Tash looked at her, surprised that Anisha had noticed how much she was clinging to her phone calls, Skype chats and emails with Mum. She thought she'd been hiding it well – she hadn't wanted to make her friends feel as if she didn't like being at school with them, and she felt a bit embarrassed about missing Mum so much. Then she realized that she shouldn't be surprised at all; Anisha was a really good friend, of course she'd noticed.

"I've been a bit…homesick, I guess."

Anisha immediately pulled her into a hug and held onto her tightly, and Tash hugged her back. Within seconds, Dani was hugging them both too.

"I wish you'd told us," said Dani. "We could have tried to help."

"I'm sorry," said Tash.

"No, don't be sorry!" said Anisha. "It's so hard being away from home. I miss my parents and my little brothers like crazy."

"Yeah, I'm lucky that I have my sister here, but I miss my parents all the time, too," added Dani. "We just have to help each other and distract each other with snowball fights and games and films in the common room."

"Thanks," Tash said giving her best friends another hug.

"We're your family, too, okay?" said Anisha, not letting her go. "So you're *not* away from home. Not really."

Chapter 7

From: twirling_tash
To: marianne.marks
Subject: Anisha

Hi Mum!

How are you?

Remember I told you that Anisha was having some problems in ballet classes? That's what caused the fight we had. Anyway, we've all made up now and everything's fine – except that I think Anisha still wishes we were working on a performance instead of an exam. It turns out she was getting so distracted because she was finding all the exam preparation boring! How can we help her get through the rest of term and remember why we're all here working so hard? Have you got any ideas? Dani and I can't think of anything!

I miss you.

Love Tash xx

From: marianne.marks
To: twirling_tash
Subject: RE: Anisha

Hi Tash darling,
I'm so glad that you and your friends worked things out and made up after your argument.

I've got to run to a meeting now but I'll send you a proper email as soon as I get a chance, and

I'll keep thinking of ideas for you to help Anisha.
Why don't you see what fun things you can do to
take her mind off dancing and the exam during
half-term?

Love Mum xxx

"Quickly, girls, enough chatting," said Miss
Anderbel at the beginning of their ballet class the
next morning.

Tash and Dani stopped whispering about how
to help Anisha fall in love with ballet again, and
Anisha turned away from her conversation with
Laura. They all faced the *barre* and started to do
pliés and stretches to warm their muscles up before
the class started properly.

"The exam is getting closer," said Miss
Anderbel. "We've got a lot to get through."

Anisha caught Tash's eye in the mirror and
pulled a face at the mention of the exam. Tash
smiled sympathetically back at her. It was so
difficult to help Anisha remember why she loved

ballet when their teachers were talking about the exam all the time.

At first, it seemed like her talk with Tash might have done the trick, as Anisha was trying harder in class. But it didn't last. Before long, she was tapping around in the corner while she waited for her turn to do an exercise, practising time steps and shuffle-hop-steps and other tap movements, even though she was just wearing her soft ballet shoes. While Miss Anderbel was talking them through exercises, or correcting people on mistakes, or telling Dani to look up because there was nothing interesting on the floor, Anisha gazed around at the rest of the class, fiddled with her hair or her leotard, pulled faces at herself in the mirror and sometimes tried to chat to the others.

She was the only one in the class who still couldn't balance in the *arabesque en pointe*, and Tash felt even more worried about Anisha doing it than she was worried about managing to do it herself. That was the exercise that everyone was dreading having to perform in the exam, but even that fear didn't seem to make Anisha concentrate. It was only a matter of time before Miss Anderbel told her off again, or maybe even called her parents in to speak to Mr Watkins, the head teacher, like she'd threatened she would.

"I'm *trying*," Anisha groaned when they were walking to their English classroom. "But even when I want to, I can't make my mind focus on ballet. It keeps wanting to do something more fun!"

"We'll help you," promised Tash. "We'll find a way." But she still didn't have any ideas.

Once everyone was busy writing poems, Dani scribbled a note to Tash on a page torn out of the back of her English book and passed it across the desk:

How do we help Anisha get through the rest of term?

Tash held the note on her lap under the table to read it. She looked up to check that Mr Kent wasn't watching and that Anisha, sitting in front of them with Donna, hadn't turned around to talk to them. Then she quietly moved the paper onto her desk and put her arm around it so that no one could see her write back:

We have to make ballet fun again.

Dani didn't bother replying on the paper. She looked at Tash with one eyebrow raised and mouthed "How?" Tash shrugged one shoulder and shook her head. That was the problem. She didn't know how to make ballet fun for Anisha, because for *her* ballet had never stopped being fun.

"We could make up funny songs to go with the exercises," suggested Dani during PE that afternoon.

She and Tash were sharing a mat to practise handstands. Anisha was sharing a mat with Donna on the other side of the gym, so Tash and Dani were trying to come up with an idea while she couldn't hear them talking about her.

"What if the songs make us laugh during the exam, though?" Tash worried.

"Yeah, maybe not," agreed Dani. "Um…okay, your turn."

"You haven't done your handstand yet!" said Tash.

"No, I meant your turn to think of an idea," said Dani.

She stepped forward and kicked her legs up into a steady handstand. While Dani was upside down, getting redder and redder in the face, Tash thought. What did Anisha like best about dancing? That was easy – performing. So they needed to remind her that performance was the point of all the hard work, just like the City Ballet dancers had said at the beginning of term.

"Maybe we'll get to go to another City Ballet performance in half-term," said Tash. "That would help Anisha remember why she loves ballet."

"But what if we don't?" said Dani, coming down from the handstand and stepping off the mat so that Tash could have a go.

Tash took her place, but stood in the middle of the small floor mat with her arms crossed. Helping Anisha was more important than practising gymnastics. "Maybe we could do some choreography. We could turn the class exercises into a proper ballet dance with characters and a story and stuff, just for us. *Or…*" she went on, her face lighting up with a better idea, "how about *not* the class exercises? We could do other types of dancing – tap, contemporary, anything but ballet practice. We'll forget about the exam and just dance for fun. It could remind Anisha why she loves dancing so much."

"Perfect!" cried Dani.

And they spent the rest of the lesson working out their plan in excited whispers.

While they were waiting in line at the canteen for dinner that evening, Tash noticed Anisha hopping up and down, practising some tap steps in her school shoes. She looked happy – much happier than she'd been in that morning's ballet class. Tash felt even more sure that their idea would work. She exchanged a grin with Dani.

"Shall we tell her?" Tash whispered, while Anisha led the way to some empty seats in the dining room after they had each filled their plates with jacket potatoes and salad.

"You tell," said Dani. "It was your idea."

"I've got a plan!" Tash said in a rush as soon as they sat down. "Let's have a dance club for the people who stay during half-term. Not ballet. Other types of dance. We can make up routines and just dance for fun!"

"I don't know," said Anisha, but her face was brightened by a hint of an excited smile. "It would be really fun…" Her face fell again. "But we're not allowed to use the studios by ourselves."

"We'll use the common room," said Tash.

"I think it's a great idea!" said Dani.

"It would be the perfect way to spend half-term," agreed Anisha. "I've been making up a tap dance, I could teach it to you."

"Plus we can do contemporary and make up dances to pop music and try out whatever new styles of dance we like," said Dani. "This is going to be the best half-term ever!"

She looked at Tash, and Tash smiled back at her, full of hope. This could be just what Anisha needed to help her fall in love with dance again.

Chapter 8

Anisha bounced up and down on the balls of her feet in the common room, eager to get the dance club started. Toril, Nick and Jonah were there too, as well as Tash and Anisha. They were all staying for half-term and as soon as they'd heard what Tash and the others were doing, they'd wanted to join in. They seemed just as excited about doing some dancing that wasn't exam preparation.

None of the Year Eights had stayed at school

for the week so they had the common room to themselves, and loads of time. After everyone who was going home for half-term had left and the school had fallen almost quiet for once, they pushed all the sofas, chairs and other clutter to the sides of the big room.

"Let's get dancing!" said Anisha. "I found some good music for a tap dance. Have you guys got tap shoes?" Everyone shook their heads.

"We can use our character shoes," said Dani.

It was a good idea – their character shoes were black, and they had a small heel, almost like tap shoes but without the taps there to make noise. They used them for learning traditional dances from other countries, which were often performed in classical ballets.

"Perfect," smiled Anisha. "I'll finish getting the middle of the room clear while you run and get your shoes."

An hour later, the main sound in the common room was laughter. Loud, constant, happy laughter. Anisha had taught everyone the beginning of a tap dance she'd made up to a song from the musical *Chicago* and then Jonah got them all laughing and pulling funny faces as they tried to move their bodies the way he showed them for a street-dance routine. They moved their legs and arms into angles they never used in ballet, jumping, turning, crouching to the floor and snapping up again, following the beat of the music.

Even though she found it difficult to get her feet to do what Jonah wanted, it was the most fun Tash had had for a long time. By the end of it she was breathless, red in the face and totally laughed-out. Her favourite move was the six-step, which was done by crouching low to the ground and crossing her feet over each other and around her body in six steps. Jonah could do it really fast. It took Tash all afternoon to learn it, but by the time they finished she could almost keep up with him.

Amazing Arabesque

From: twirling_tash
To: marianne.marks
Subject: Dance club

Hi Mum!

I'm having a great half-term so far! It's only the first day but we've already started a dance club and learned two dances. Jonah taught us to do some street dance, and Anisha's teaching us a tap dance. Anisha and I had a tap dance-off as well, where we each kept doing steps that the other one had to copy, making them harder and harder and trying to catch each other out. Anisha won, of course, because she's so good – it was so much fun! I hope that our idea really does make her feel better about everything.

I hope you're having a good week too!

Love Tash xx

All week they worked on the two dances, and Tash could see that the plan was working. Anisha was much, much happier. She laughed and smiled, and when they were dancing, she was totally focused on getting the street-dance steps right and helping the others to learn her tap routine. They watched videos of dance routines from *Strictly Come Dancing* on YouTube too and tried to copy the moves for the jive and the waltz, whirling around the room in pairs, stepping on each other's toes, bumping into the furniture and falling onto the sofas with cries of laughter.

"I've had such a great week," said Anisha on Sunday afternoon. "I wish we could dance like this all the time."

"Ballet will be just as much fun when the exam's over, you know," said Tash.

"Try this one with me," Nick said to Anisha, showing them both a jive move in the video where the man lifted the woman, dipped her low to the ground and then swung her back up again while she kicked her legs high into the air.

"Nooo way," said Anisha. "You'll drop me."

"I won't!" insisted Nick. "I'm a ballet dancer. I'm *trained* to lift you."

Anisha snorted. "You're *being* trained to lift me. You've never actually done it yet."

"Let's just try," said Nick, and Anisha grinned and gave in.

They watched the video clip a few more times to see how it was done, then they stood ready, facing each other. Nick had his hands on Anisha's waist and she put hers on his shoulders. Tash leaned against the wall, smiling as she watched.

"One..." Anisha counted, "two..."

The door banged open and Donna and Laura stood staring at them.

"What are you guys doing?" they demanded.

Jonah, Dani and Toril were crouched down with one leg kicked out to the front, halfway through the street-dance routine. Anisha and Nick had chickened out of the jive move and were laughing.

"Dance club," said Anisha.

"Sounds great!" Laura said immediately. "Can we join?"

"It was just for half-term, really," explained Dani.

"Let's keep it going!" said Anisha. "After school and at weekends and stuff."

"Yes!" cried everyone all at once.

Tash grinned over at Anisha. Half-term might be over, but dance club definitely wasn't.

By the end of the evening, word had spread and quite a few other people in their class and in Year Eight had asked to join the dance club, too. Tash was thrilled, especially because she hoped it would mean that Anisha would carry on being as happy as she'd been all week. But she was a bit worried, too. After breaking the school rules in her first term had led to such a horrible accident and serious trouble with the teachers, Tash really didn't want to do anything that wasn't allowed.

"I think we should check with Miss Dixon about making dance club official," she said, worrying that the head of Year Seven and Eight would be angry if she found out they were doing something like this without her permission.

"But what if she says we're not allowed?" asked Anisha.

Tash frowned. "It would be worse if we did it without asking and then got caught," she said.

"Let's ask her now," said Dani. "Then we'll know for sure."

They went to find Miss Dixon, who was talking to Lily-May's parents in Clara dorm, the other Year Seven dormitory. They hung around in the corridor until she'd finished.

"Hi, girls," Miss Dixon said as she left the room. "Did you want something?"

"Yes," said Dani immediately, and Miss Dixon laughed at her directness.

"We've been making up some dances in the common room..." said Tash. "We'd really like to carry on doing it for the rest of term, like a dance club."

"Lots of people want to join in," said Anisha.

"We *promise* we'll still work hard for the ballet exam. And we'll all do our homework and everything."

"Well," said Miss Dixon, considering it. "As long as you're careful not to get injured, I think it should be fine. I don't want you using the common room to dance, though. Not if there's going to be a big group of you. You can use one of the studios, if you can get one of your dance teachers to supervise you. And I want a list of everyone who's taking part – if anyone's schoolwork slips because they don't have enough time for homework, then they'll have to stop."

"Yesss!" said Dani.

Anisha said, "Thank you, thank you, thank you!" at the same time and Tash just smiled. It was official: dance club was on!

They spent an hour making a poster; Anisha drew pictures to represent different types of dance –

figures doing street dance, and swing dance, tap shoes and music notes – and they wrote "Year Seven and Eight Dance Club" across the top in funky letters and "NO BALLET ALLOWED" at the bottom. They stuck it on the inside of the common room door and put another piece of paper next to it for people to sign up so that they could give the list to Miss Dixon later. Anisha wrote her own name down first, followed by Tash and Dani. By the time they all went to bed, the piece of paper was full of names. Almost everyone from Year Seven and half of Year Eight had signed up.

"I guess you're not the only one who thinks dancing needs to be more fun this term," Tash said to Anisha while they stood side by side, brushing their teeth.

"I know why you started the dance club, Tash," said Anisha.

She paused and Tash wondered if Anisha was annoyed with her for interfering again.

"You're the best," she said.

Chapter 9

Tash, Dani and Anisha stayed behind after their morning ballet class the next day to tell Miss Anderbel about their dance club.

"It sounds like fun," she said. "Just be careful that nobody gets injured."

"We'll be really safe," promised Tash. "But there is one thing we wanted to ask... Could we use one of the studios? Miss Dixon said we can't use the common room, so we won't be able to keep the club going otherwise."

"You know you're not allowed to use the

studios without a teacher until you're in Year Ten," said Miss Anderbel, looking sternly at Tash, who had broken that rule the term before.

"We know…" said Anisha. "We were hoping… maybe…one of the teachers might not mind supervising…"

"Just for an hour or something, maybe a couple of times a week?" added Dani.

"Okay, I'll see when I have some free evenings and book one of the studios for you," agreed Miss Anderbel. "I'm pleased to see that you want to dance in your spare time, too!"

"Thanks!" Tash, Dani and Anisha said together.

The first proper dance-club session was the next evening. After everyone had eaten dinner and done some homework, they gathered in the studio that Miss Anderbel had found for them. A lot of people had turned up and they were all dressed in casual dance clothes, some of them holding character shoes or jazz shoes, some just in socks or bare feet. The room was buzzing with excited chatter while everyone warmed their muscles up with some stretches. Some people were already trying out some tap steps and others were whirling each other around in pretend waltzes.

"What shall we do today?" asked Dani, clapping her hands to get everyone's attention.

"Hands up for a tap dance!" said Tash, shooting her own arm into the air, followed quickly by Dani and Anisha.

Lots of other people put their hands up, too, and Tash quickly counted. "Okay, that's twenty. Who wants to do street dance?" More hands went up and Tash counted them again. "Twelve. Tap wins for tonight!"

"I could teach everyone the dance we did in half-term," offered Anisha.

Everyone agreed, so they all grabbed their character shoes and found a space to dance, and Anisha began to show them the moves. It was harder with more people because everyone had less room, but doing tap steps on the studio floor sounded much better than on the carpet in the common room.

Miss Anderbel was there to supervise, but she didn't act like a teacher at all. She sat down at the piano with a book and didn't interfere with what they were doing, but Tash noticed that she didn't turn many pages. She was too busy watching the dancers trying out new steps and going over their routines.

With only five minutes before they all had to go and have showers before bed, Dani hesitantly asked if anyone wanted to do a contemporary dance.

"I know we do contemporary class properly," she said. "But I was working on a dance over Christmas and it would be cool to try it out on you guys. If you want."

"Let's see!" demanded Anisha, and everyone agreed. "Show us now, and we can start working on it next time."

Dani plugged her iPod into the speakers they were using and selected a slow, sad pop song that everyone knew. They cleared a space for her and when the music started she began to dance beautiful steps. There were a few places where she stopped to explain what a group of dancers would do, and Tash could picture it working perfectly with five or six people. Dani was a good dancer, but Tash was amazed that she'd made this dance up all by herself. It was almost like something Miss Carter, their contemporary dance teacher, would choreograph. Everyone clapped when she finished and Dani smiled widely, bounding back to Tash's side.

"What do you think?" she asked anxiously.

"That was good!" said Tash. "*So* good."

"Miss Anderbel will be amazed that you didn't choreograph the whole thing to be danced looking at the floor," teased Anisha, checking over her shoulder to make sure their teacher wasn't listening.

"Oooh, that's a *great* idea!" joked Dani.

"Can I be in it if I promise to look down the whole time?" laughed Tash.

"Oh, me too! Me too!" said Anisha, and she hung her head pretending to be sad and poetic.

"Shut up," giggled Dani. "And you two had better be in it!"

Everyone filed out, chatting about how much fun they'd had.

"That dance was so good, Dani!" said Toril. "I really liked this bit…" And she started to move her arms, trying to copy what Dani had done as they walked through the changing room and outside to go back to the main school building.

"Well," Tash said to Anisha as they headed up to Coppélia with the others. "It's official: dance club is a hit!"

From: twirling_tash
To: marianne.marks
Subject: RE: RE: Dance club

Hi Mum,

Dance club is brilliant!

This evening Dani started to teach us the contemporary dance she's made up. I can see even more now how dancing just for fun is making Anisha really happy. I even noticed her practising a few ballet steps while Dani was explaining something to Laura, so I think the plan is working!

Gotta go now.

Love you!

Tash xx

Miss Anderbel agreed to let them use the studio again on Wednesday evenings and Saturday afternoons as well as Monday evenings and she and Miss Carter took turns supervising. On Wednesday, they went through the tap and street-dance routines again a few times, and Dani began to teach them all the contemporary dance. Tash loved the steps Dani had made up and she was still practising them as everyone started to leave at the end of the session.

"Will the rest of the school get to see any of your work?" Miss Anderbel asked, coming up to Tash, Dani and Anisha when they were the only people left in the studio. The three friends looked at each other.

"That's a brilliant idea!" gushed Anisha, glowing with excitement. "That's the one thing that could make dance club *even more amazing*."

"Could we do a performance?" asked Tash.

"Yes! Please?" begged Dani and Anisha.

"At the end of term," added Dani.

"Can we use the school stage like we did at the Christmas fair?" asked Anisha.

"I'm afraid the stage isn't mine to promise to you," said Miss Anderbel. "You'll have to ask Mr Watkins."

Their faces fell. Mr Watkins was the head teacher and he could be pretty scary. All of them remembered having to talk to him and answer his questions at their audition for the school.

"Good luck!" added Miss Anderbel, and she gave them an encouraging smile.

Tash looked at the clock on the wall. It was much too late to ask Mr Watkins now; they'd have to wait until the next morning.

"I don't know, girls," Mr Watkins said, when Anisha had told him about dance club and asked if they could use the stage for a performance. "It mustn't interfere with your preparation for the end-of-term ballet exam."

"I think it will *help* with the ballet exam!" Tash burst out.

"How do you mean?" Mr Watkins asked.

"We're working so, so hard for the exam, but we need to have some fun, too. I learned that last term." Tash couldn't help going a bit pink as she spoke, remembering the last time she'd been in Mr Watkins' office. Her injury the previous term had won her a stern lecture from him. "The dance club is just going to be *fun* and we think it'll help us to stop worrying...so much...about things..." she trailed off awkwardly.

Mr Watkins looked at each of them carefully, considering the idea, and they all looked hopefully back at him.

"Well, I have to say, I'm pleased to see that our youngest students are so keen to choreograph their own work," he said. "And as you're all putting so much effort into it, it would be a great shame not to have a performance. It would go against everything that this school is here to teach you!"

They waited until they were on the other side of the door – after they'd thanked and thanked Mr Watkins – to high-five each other in a little circle. Then they hurried off to form time. They were a bit late, but everyone knew where they'd been, including Mr Kent, apparently. Tash gave Jonah a little grin and two thumbs up, as she walked quickly to her seat next to Toril. As soon as Mr Kent continued with what he'd been saying, Laura tapped Tash on the shoulder and asked her in a whisper what Mr Watkins had said. Donna was asking Dani the same thing, and out of the corner of her eye Tash could see Rob asking Anisha.

"Let's all hear what happened, shall we?" said Mr Kent, and Tash turned guiltily back round in her seat. But Mr Kent was smiling. "Come on, you three," he said. "Give us a re-enactment."

Everyone laughed, and Tash turned to look uncertainly at Anisha. But Anisha was already on her feet and heading to the front of the classroom, with Dani following. Tash shrugged at Laura and went with them, and seconds later everyone was laughing as Anisha did an impression of Mr Watkins that was so spot-on Tash wondered if they should include some comedy in their dance-club performance. The whole class applauded when they'd finished and, from the smiles on everyone's faces, Tash could tell that they were also celebrating the fact that the dance club would get to perform to the school.

Amazing Arabesque

By Saturday, everyone had learned the steps of the tap routine and they were halfway through Jonah's street dance. It was so much fun practising the quick, rhythmic tap steps in the school's largest dance studio, with its big mirrors and hard floor perfect for tapping.

The tap steps sounded wonderful, loud and snappy, even though most of them were only dancing in character shoes. Being able to hear the taps made it obvious where some people hadn't got the hang of the rhythm yet, but Anisha, Tash, Jonah and the others who'd done tap lessons before coming to Aurora House were happy to help their friends get it right.

The street dance was going well, too. Tash couldn't help laughing when she saw herself doing it in the mirror. It was so different to ballet! Ballet was all about turnout and a straight back – street dance was free, and there weren't set positions like in ballet. At first, Tash had found it weird and difficult to throw off her ballet training and move in a different way, but now she was starting to get it. And when they all did the moves together, in perfect time with each other and the beat of the music – even when they did the fast six-step – it was so exciting! She almost felt like a different person. She could never love anything as much as she loved ballet, but dancing like this was great, too.

Keeping in mind Mr Watkins' warning about the ballet exam, they decided that nobody would perform in all three dances – tap, street dance and contemporary. Dani immediately chose to drop out of her own contemporary piece and just teach it to the others.

"I'll be nervous enough just knowing that people are watching my choreography," she admitted to Tash. "I don't want to have to worry about messing up the steps as well!"

Anisha was obviously going to do the tap dance, as she was by far the best tap dancer in the group, and she'd already promised Dani that she'd be in her contemporary piece. Tash had promised too, so that left a choice between Anisha's tap routine and Jonah's street dance. She agonized over it for an entire day – she'd finally managed to get the hang of the street-dance moves and she was pleased with herself – but in the end she chose to be in Anisha's dance. The thing that would make her most proud in the dance-club performance would be to dance two routines choreographed by her best friends.

Chapter 10

Tash had spent so much time thinking about how to help Anisha that she'd forgotten to worry about the other things that had been bothering her this term. But there was one thing she hadn't forgotten about: her birthday.

Dance club had helped her feel better about everything, but even that couldn't stop her from missing Mum and home whenever she thought about her birthday. It was only days away now and already a parcel had arrived from Mum and another one from Maddy. She'd put them in the little chest of drawers next to her bed and decided not to open them until her actual birthday, but it was hard to resist shaking them and trying to guess what was under the pretty wrapping paper.

"Ooh, birthday presents!" said Dani when she saw them the night before Tash's birthday. "Exciting!"

"Yeah," said Tash. "They're from my mum and my friend Maddy. But I wish they could see me open them! And I won't get to say thank you to them properly, except on the phone after school – hours and hours after I've opened the presents."

"I bet your birthday will still be exciting though," said Anisha, and Tash saw her glance at Dani and try to hide a small giggle. Dani glared at Anisha and gave her a tiny kick on the ankle, which Tash also spotted.

"I doubt it," said Tash. "If it was at the weekend

we could go to the cinema or something, but it's a school day. So that means it'll just be ballet and school and character dance and school dinner and homework."

"You never know…" Anisha said with a grin, which caused Dani to give her another weird look.

"What's up with you two?" Tash asked suspiciously.

"Time for bed!" cried Dani, diving under her covers before Tash could ask her anything else. Tash laughed and settled down in her own bed. She wondered what her first ballet-school birthday would be like.

Tash was woken up by an extra early alarm the next morning. She'd set her own alarm fifteen minutes earlier than usual so that she'd have time to open the presents before breakfast, but the sound that woke her up wasn't the familiar beeping of her phone. The first thing she was aware of was a strange feeling of longing, which felt like it was coming from her insides all the way up into her head – longing for home and for Mum, for a warm cuddle and to hear Mum say "Happy birthday, darling" like she'd woken up to on every birthday she'd ever had.

Half asleep and trying to push her homesickness away, she wondered if the alarm she could hear was a fire drill and thought, if it was, it would be the worst start to a birthday in the whole history of birthdays. But it wasn't. It was Dani's alarm and it was half an hour earlier than they usually woke up. Tash sat up in bed, wondering what was going on. To her surprise, everyone else was sitting up, too.

She looked around the room. There was a banner above the door that said "Happy birthday" in sparkly letters and a big pink helium balloon by Tash's bed. The others had covered the wardrobe that she and Dani shared with glittery streamers, and strung more of them across the end of her bed and the little bedside chest of drawers. Someone had even thrown sparkly happy birthday confetti on her bed while she slept.

"Happy birthday!" they all said in unison with big smiles on their faces, clearly enjoying every second of Tash's surprise.

"How did you keep all this a secret?" she asked, tugging on the pink ribbon that hung down from the balloon. It was weighted down by a pink plastic star that bobbed along the floor by her bed when she moved the ribbon.

"We hid it all under Laura's bed," giggled Dani.

"We thought you'd *never* fall asleep last night!" said Anisha. "We waited until we could hear you snoring to set all this up."

Tash laughed. "It's perfect," she said. She let go of the ribbon and watched the balloon bob up and down crazily. "I love it, thank you!"

She smiled at everyone. Then she reached into her drawer to pick up the presents from Mum and Maddy. When she sat back up again, Dani was sitting on the end of her bed holding out a card, a small gift and a cupcake with pink icing and a candle. They hadn't been able to light the candle, so someone had made a pretend flame from coloured crêpe paper and stuck it to the top of the candle with Sellotape. Tash laughed and pretended to blow it out, pulling the crêpe paper off the candle as she did so.

"From all of us," said Dani, holding the present out to her.

The others got out of bed too and came over. Dani scooted up to sit next to Tash under the covers, while Laura and Toril sat on the end, wrapping one of the blankets from Tash's bed around their shoulders. Anisha sat on her own bed and Donna came and joined her. Tash looked at the card first.

"Anisha drew the picture," said Donna.

"It's beautiful," said Tash, running her fingertips over the drawing of a ballet dancer that she guessed was meant to be her, dressed in a lovely blue tutu, because blue was her favourite colour, and performing an *arabesque en pointe*. She opened the card and started to read all the messages the others had written for her.

"Oh my God, open the present!" said Dani, shoving the gift, wrapped in light blue crêpe paper from the art room, under her face.

Tash laughed and took it from Dani. It felt soft in her hands and she couldn't work out what it might be. She tore the paper off and unfolded a pretty, flowery cloth bag with a drawstring at the top.

"It's to keep your pointe shoes in," said Laura.

"See, there's a label," said Toril, pulling out a tag that was attached to the string. It said "Tash's beautiful shoes for beautiful dancing" in Toril's neat handwriting.

"We got it from the dance shop in town so it's the perfect size," added Donna. "Helen and her friends took us shopping."

Amazing Arabesque

"So *that's* where you, Toril and Laura disappeared to the weekend before last! I kept wondering where you were – no wonder Dani and Anisha kept giggling when I asked!"

"Do you like it?" asked Dani. "We wanted to make sure your birthday would be really special."

"I *love* it. And I love you all. Thanks, you guys. You're the best."

Tash opened the presents from Mum and Maddy while the others got dressed. Maddy had sent her a book and a little bottle of sparkly blue nail varnish. Tash would only be able to wear it at weekends because it wasn't allowed in ballet classes or school lessons, but it was lovely of Maddy to send it and Tash couldn't wait to hang out with her in the Easter holidays and paint their nails as much as they liked.

Inside the pretty wrapping paper and ribbon on Mum's present was a ballet DVD and a new dress. Tash looked at the DVD, a City Ballet performance of *Cinderella*. There was a piece of card lying inside the wrapping paper with something written on it in Mum's loopy, slanted handwriting: "This card entitles my wonderful Tash and her best friends Dani and Anisha to one very late birthday surprise on the last day of term." Tash turned the card over but there were no clues as to what the surprise might be.

"Look!" she said to Dani and Anisha, passing them the card so they could read it.

"That's so cool!" said Anisha.

"I wonder what it will be..." said Dani. She hugged Tash excitedly and then flung out an arm to pull Anisha in too. They all jumped up and down happily for a minute and then Tash really had to hurry into her leotard, tights and school tracksuit if she was going to make it downstairs in time for breakfast.

Tash's teachers and the rest of her year all said happy birthday to her in lessons, and in her ballet class she felt like she was dancing better than ever. It was as if the special morning with her friends had given her extra sparkle and made her jumps higher, her footwork sharper and her balances more precise. When they got to pointe work, she actually managed to hold a balance in *arabesque* for two whole seconds! And Anisha seemed to be working harder than ever, too. Tash wondered if the lovely morning in Coppélia had reminded her how much she wanted to pass the exam and stay in their year group.

"Well, Tash, I think your feet are stronger now than they were before your injury," said Miss Downing at lunchtime, when Tash had gone through each of the physio exercises once. "You don't need any more physio. You can have your lunchtimes back."

"Thank you!" cried Tash and she was still so full of birthday joy that she couldn't help giving Miss Downing a hug.

"Just be careful in future."

"I will," promised Tash. "So…I can go now?"

"Yes," laughed Miss Downing. "Go and enjoy the rest of break."

Tash ran out of the room and dashed down the stairs. She'd seen Dani and Anisha out on the school field from the window so she ran to find them and gave them both a big hug.

"No more physio!" she said. "This birthday is my favourite one ever."

"It's not over yet," smiled Anisha.

In form time after lunch, Mr Kent produced a chocolate cake with brightly coloured hundreds and thousands all over the top, and cut it into delicious slices. Tash handed them round with a big smile, feeling so glad that all these people shared a school and home with her every day.

In between the character dance class and dinner, Tash went up to Coppélia to phone Mum. She couldn't stop talking about how special her birthday had been and how amazing her friends were.

Amazing Arabesque

"I'm glad you had a nice day," said Mum. "I wish I could have seen you to give you your present myself."

"Thanks for the presents," said Tash. "I love them. Thanks for the surprise, too, even though I don't know what it is yet!"

Mum laughed. "You're welcome, darling. I can't wait to see you at the end of term and take you out for your special birthday treat."

"Me too," said Tash. "I can show you the present my friends gave me. And my pointe shoes!"

"You sound much happier," said Mum.

"I am," replied Tash. She looked up at the birthday banner above the door, and stood up on her bed so that she could see her reflection in the shiny pink balloon. "I still miss you, but I love living at Aurora House, and I love dancing every day, and I really, really love my friends."

"I'm so pleased your friends have helped you feel better about things," said Mum.

Tash smiled at her pink reflection. Anisha and

Dani were the best friends ever, and they'd made her birthday so wonderful and helped her to see that, even though she was far away from Mum and home, she was part of the Aurora House family now. Dani poked her head around the door and mimed eating dinner.

"Gotta go!" Tash said to Mum. "It's time for dinner."

"Happy birthday," said Mum. "I love you."

"Love you!" Tash said, jumping off the bed. "Bye!"

By the evening Tash's face almost hurt from smiling so much. After dinner, she, Dani and Anisha dashed through their homework, leaving as much for the next day as they possibly could and then settled into the sofa in the common room to watch Tash's new ballet DVD. As Tash let the gorgeous *Cinderella* music fill her whole body, she longed for the day when she could dance like the City Ballet dancers. While Dani and Anisha passed comments about the steps and the dancers to each other, Tash allowed herself to be completely drawn in to the ballet.

"Look! That's Christine who came to our class!" said Dani.

"It isn't," said Anisha.

"It *is!*"

When she'd opened the present, Tash had felt a tiny bit sad that she wouldn't get to watch the DVD with Mum until the Easter holidays, but now she realized that watching it with her friends was even better. Mum would probably enjoy it, but she wouldn't *get* it like they did.

"Ohhh, look at that," gasped Anisha. "I want to do that."

"Do you think we could?" Dani asked, getting up to try.

"Sit down, you're blocking my view!" laughed Anisha. "This bit's amazing."

"I could do it, I totally could. If only I could see it a bit slower…"

"And if you could dance *en pointe* without the *barre*."

"Well, *obviously*, I meant I could do it in flat shoes."

"Tash, you could do it, couldn't you?" insisted Dani, sitting down again between Tash and Anisha. "I bet you could."

Tash smiled at her friends, thinking, *Yep, best birthday ever.*

The end of term was approaching fast. But now, when Tash counted the days left at school, she wasn't desperately inching closer to seeing Mum, she was adding up how many dance-club practices they had left and feeling the excitement of their performance growing greater every day. She couldn't wait to show the rest of the school what they'd done, all by themselves. But that was just a bonus on top of the thrill that rushed through her whenever she thought about stepping onto the stage with her friends, knowing that this was their one chance to give their dances absolutely everything they had. It was her favourite feeling in the world.

From: marianne.marks
To: twirling_tash
Subject: Hello

Hi Tash,

Is everything okay? I haven't had an email or a phone call from you for a while. I hope it's just because you're too busy having fun and not because there's something wrong.

I'm looking forward to hearing more about your dance club.

Love Mum xx

From: twirling_tash
To: marianne.marks
Subject: RE: Hello

Hi Mum,

I'm sooo sorry that I didn't email you back until now! I'm so busy with dance club at the moment – it's going great. I really think it's helping Anisha to feel better about dancing. And guess what? It's helped me too! I've got so much to think about now with the dances we're making up and organizing our end of term performance, and of course there's the ballet exam too – I just don't have time to feel so homesick any more. Isn't that brilliant?

Love Tash xx

She wasn't the only one that dance club worked its magic on. Anisha was so much happier that Tash knew it must be obvious to everyone, even the people who hadn't realized how she'd been feeling before. She was getting told off by Miss Anderbel way less, too. Tash thought that she and Dani were probably just as relieved as Anisha was about that.

"Hey, this step is kind of like that one in Dani's

dance, isn't it?" Anisha murmured to Tash while they were standing in the corner of the studio waiting for their turn in an exercise of *balancés* and *pirouettes* that travelled across the floor. "I mean, hers is a more contemporary version. But it's the same idea."

"Yeah, it is," smiled Tash. And then they were off, gliding and spinning across the room, as light as air. Tash couldn't see what Anisha was doing but her friend earned a *"Lovely*, Anisha!" from Miss Anderbel.

Towards the end of the lesson they all changed their flat ballet shoes for their pointe shoes, which were no longer quite as pink or shiny as they had been at the beginning of term. Tash put hers on as quickly as she could and then went to the *barre* to warm her feet up. Today they were going to dance in the centre, finally! They practised the three *barre* exercises for the exam first – rises and *relevés* and stepping up into low *arabesques* while holding on to the *barre*, and then letting go to prove they could balance. The *arabesque* was still the most difficult thing they'd have to do in the exam, but Tash felt like she was really getting better at it. She could almost always balance for a few seconds when she let go of the *barre*, and she was starting to worry a lot less about the exam.

Out of the corner of her eye, she saw Anisha come down from the *arabesque* balance far too early. She was definitely trying harder now, but she still had a lot of catching up to do.

"I'll never be able to do it," she muttered to Tash.

"Just keep trying, you're getting better," Tash whispered back.

"Find a space in the centre," said Miss Anderbel, when they'd finished. "Let's start with some more *relevés*."

Tash and the others quickly arranged themselves into three lines across the middle of the studio.

Amazing Arabesque

"You've all been doing so well at pointe work at the *barre* that we've decided to include two very short centre exercises in your exam."

Tash gasped and looked around at the rest of the class. The exam had suddenly become scary again!

"Don't panic!" smiled Miss Anderbel, seeing their faces. "I know you can do it."

Even though *relevés* were basic steps, trying them *en pointe* in the centre was still exciting – and a bit nerve-racking, too. Tash always tried not to hold onto the *barre* too tightly but she was used to having it there to stop her falling. Without it, she'd have to hold herself steady using pure strength from her stomach muscles and her legs.

The exercise was similar to the one they did at the *barre*, standing in fifth position and then quickly rising onto pointe by drawing both feet snappily together, one foot tightly crossed in front of the other, and then lowering quickly back down. She tried one while Miss Anderbel explained the exercise and a surprised grin broke out across her face. She could do it! It felt wonderful, so she did another one and then another, and then tried to use her arms, too. Soon everyone was trying and all around her, Tash could hear small thuds and clops as the class worked out how to come down neatly.

They did them to second position, too, sliding their feet out and up at the same time so that they stood on their toes with their legs apart. They didn't really have to balance much because *relevés* were so quick and they only did very short sequences. The steps were quite simple, but Tash felt as if she was making progress at last. Somehow it felt more like dancing when you were in the centre and could use your arms and your head and change direction while you did the steps. Even though she'd been a bit annoyed about spending so much of the term doing pointe work at the *barre*, it had made her feet strong and she was able to do the exercise in the centre without wobbling. It was an amazing feeling.

Next, they learned to *couru*, a movement that was supposed to look as if you were gliding across the floor, taking lots and lots of tiny little steps and keeping your feet and legs pressed together in fifth position as much as possible. They did them across the room with their arms rounded above their heads and Tash watched herself in the mirror. It was painful; out of all the steps they'd learned so far, this simple one was the one that hurt the most. But she watched herself doing it and saw she looked graceful, as if it was the easiest thing in the world. She felt like she was properly dancing in her pointe shoes for the first time. Her toes were killing her, but at the same time, nothing had ever felt better.

Dancing *en pointe* in the Aurora House studios where the bright sunshine from the high windows cast golden patches on the floor, with her friends dancing all around her perfectly in time as if they were a real *corps de ballet* in a real ballet company, she knew she wouldn't want to be anywhere else. She watched Anisha, and her friend looked as if she was skimming across clouds, wearing a lovely sunny smile. Whether or not Anisha knew it, the upcoming dance-club performance was making her try harder at *all* her dancing. Tash just hoped that it would be enough to make up for the first half of the term, and to get her through the exam. They only had a week to go.

Chapter 11

Tash's class had their ballet exam on the last Monday morning of term. How they'd been doing in their contemporary, character dance and *pas de deux* classes so far would be considered by their teachers, too, but classical ballet was the only class where they had an actual exam. Having the exam first thing on a Monday morning was supposed to mean that they were all rested and full of energy after the weekend, but of course everyone had spent the whole weekend worrying.

With less than twenty-four hours to go until exam time, they persuaded Miss Anderbel to let them have an extra dance-club rehearsal on Sunday afternoon. Tash was gladder than ever that they could all turn their worries into a completely different kind of dancing.

"Perfect, Anisha!" said Dani while they were practising the contemporary dance. "Tash, can you move your arm down a little so you're not blocking Lily-May's face? That's better…okay… the bit in the circle is fine…let's go over the ending again."

Dani was being especially picky about the contemporary dance today and Tash wondered if it was because her exam stress was coming out as dance-club worries. But Tash thought that Dani didn't need to worry about the contemporary dance at all. Things were going well at dance club – really, really well. Even if the contemporary dance hadn't been made up by her best friend,

Amazing Arabesque

Tash would have thought it was brilliant.

They moved onto the tap dance next. Now that everyone had completely got the steps, dancing it was one of the most fun things Tash had ever done. She was so proud of what their dance club had achieved with just their own ideas, and she couldn't wait to show the rest of the school. She hoped they'd be impressed. But now it was time to impress someone else: her ballet teachers.

Six alarms went off early in Coppélia on Monday morning. For once, they were all out of bed almost instantly. Tash was too nervous to sleep anyway, and she'd been lying awake for fifteen minutes already, going through ballet steps in her mind and reminding herself of all the things Miss Anderbel usually corrected people on.

"I'm nervous," admitted Dani, the first one to say it out loud.

"You and the whole school," said Laura, wriggling into her pale-pink ballet tights.

"We'll be fine," said Donna with what sounded like confidence. "Right?"

Anisha and Tash exchanged anxious looks with each other. Anisha sat down glumly on the bed, dressed in her leotard and tights, her hairbrush hanging limply from her hand.

"Right," Tash agreed, forcing her voice to sound bright like Donna's. She looked at her friends' reflections in the mirror as she pushed hairpins into her dark hair to hold it in a bun. "We know the exercises. We do them well every day. This won't be any different."

"I *don't* know them!" wailed Dani, flopping backwards onto her bed where she'd been sitting while she pulled her light-blonde hair up into a ponytail. "I've forgotten everything!"

"No, you haven't," insisted Tash, going over to her friend. She grabbed Dani's hands and pulled her upright again. "You're just nervous. Once the music starts you'll be *fine*." Dani smiled slightly and nodded, then she went to share the mirror with Toril to finish doing her hair. Tash crawled across her own bed to sit next to Anisha on hers. "You're going to be fine, too," Tash said seriously. Anisha nodded silently. She'd hadn't spoken once since she'd got out of bed.

"I hope so," she whispered. "Oh, Tash, why didn't I work harder?" she cried, covering her face with her hands.

"It's been a difficult term," said Tash, putting her arm around Anisha and pulling her closer, as if she could transfer some of her own confidence to her friend that way. "For both of us."

"I won't be able to do the *arabesque*. I know I won't. I don't want to have to repeat Year Seven!" Anisha said, dropping her hands into her lap and looking down at them.

"The *arabesque* exercise isn't everything. You're a good dancer," Tash said. Anisha looked doubtful. "You *are*. And our teachers know that. You had some bad classes this term but if you go into the exam and try the hardest you've ever tried, and put as much love into your ballet steps as you do into the dance-club routines, they're going to see how great you are."

"Okay," Anisha nodded. "You're right. I hope."

"Trust me," said Tash, making a silent wish that she *was* right and that Anisha's bad term wouldn't ruin her chances of staying in their class. "So stop worrying and give me your hairbrush."

Anisha laughed and handed it over. Tash kneeled up on the bed behind her and pulled the brush through Anisha's long, black hair. She put it into a ponytail, and then twisted it up into a bun, and Anisha sat up straighter and straighter with every second that passed, so that by the time her hair was in a perfect ballet dancer's bun, Anisha was the picture of a perfect ballet dancer too.

Tash spent all of breakfast repeating to her friends and herself that the exam would be just like any other morning ballet class. But as soon as they arrived at the school's small theatre, where the exams were taking place, she could see that it wasn't. They were doing the exam in groups of three, and the first group in the whole school to go in front of the teachers was Tash, Dani and Anisha. There was a table at the front of the little auditorium with glasses of water, pads of paper and pens and three chairs set out behind it. One for Miss Anderbel, obviously, and who else?

Miss Anderbel was shuffling some papers around on the table as the girls came in and stood awkwardly in the middle of the stage.

"Find a space at the *barre* and warm up, please," said Miss Anderbel.

They went to the portable *barre* in the middle of the stage, where they stood, Tash and Dani on one side and Anisha on the other, nervously warming up their muscles and chatting quietly. The door opened again and Mr Edwards, their *pas de deux* teacher, walked in and smiled at them before taking a seat at the table. *One seat left*, thought Tash, and then the door opened again and she saw Mr Watkins. Tash looked at Dani in alarm and got a look of terror back from her friend. Mr Watkins was the most important teacher at the school and he was here to watch them dance and to decide if they could move up to Year Eight next year or had to stay in Year Seven.

Fear rushed up through every muscle of Tash's body. She'd been so busy trying to make Anisha feel more confident and trying to reassure Dani and the others, that she hadn't thought about her own nervousness. It had been hidden under layers of pretence that everything was going to be fine – but now it was right at the top, shivering in her hands and her feet and blanking out everything that she remembered about the exercises for this class.

"I know this is your first ballet exam at Aurora House," said Mr Watkins. "But try to forget that we're here, and just dance the best you can."

"Easy for him to say, right?" said Miss Anderbel, and everyone laughed.

Tash smiled at her teacher and Miss Anderbel,

catching her eye, smiled back. Tash took a deep breath. This was it. The nervous laughter faded from the room and it seemed to take some of Tash's anxiety with it. She placed her hand on the *barre*. She was ready.

Miss Anderbel talked them through the exam from her seat at the front, telling them which exercises to do even though they all knew the order anyway. Tash held tightly on to the *barre* to stop her hand from shaking, and she hoped that her other hand, the one that was moving through the air in the set positions of the exercises, wasn't shaking so much that the teachers could see it. This was her one big chance to show her teachers everything that she'd learned at Aurora House so far.

She had missed out on the Christmas performance, so this was her first time dancing on the school's small stage. It wasn't like a normal ballet class at all. There were no mirrors, so Tash couldn't check that her legs and arms and feet were placed correctly. She had to rely on the way the steps felt and trust her body to do them right. It was scary. Every time she looked up and out to the front, she saw a wave of empty tiered seats, and at the front, the three stern examiners, scribbling down notes about every little thing she was doing. She was desperate to know what they were writing. Were they pleased with the way she did *developpés*? Were they horrified by her *ronds de jambes*? She was used to hearing Miss Anderbel correct things that were wrong, but all their teacher was saying this morning were the names of the exercises. Tash couldn't help worrying that she might be making mistakes right now and not even know it. It was a horrible thought.

But just hearing Miss Anderbel's familiar voice helped, and each time they turned around to do the exercises on the other leg, and Tash was facing the back of the stage, she could almost forget that

Mr Watkins and Mr Edwards were there too. Tash's confidence grew and grew as her body moved through the exercises that she knew so well, so that by the time they got to *grands battements*, if she'd had to tell her friends that everything was going to be fine, she wouldn't even be pretending. She wanted to impress her teachers, but she'd worked hard in ballet all term, and she knew that she could dance these exercises well. She started to enjoy herself as much as she enjoyed every ballet class, doing it just for the incredible floating-on-air feeling she got from dancing. As she danced, she noticed that Dani was performing beautifully with her eyes up and a smile on her face, and that Anisha was dancing well, too. Seeing that made her feel even better.

Right at the end of the exam, they had a few minutes to have a drink and put their pointe shoes on. The three girls gathered in a tight circle at the back of the stage and tied the ribbons on their shoes.

"I wish we didn't have to do pointe work!" whispered Dani.

"Me too," whispered Anisha. "I bet I'm going to fall over!"

"Good luck!" Tash whispered. She grabbed Dani's and Anisha's hands and gave them a quick squeeze. They all looked at each other. "We can do this."

Dani and Anisha nodded and squeezed hands one more time. Then they stood up and went back to their places.

Even though it was an exam and she was about to be judged on whether or not she could do the short pointe work exercises they'd learned, Tash couldn't help a little thrill at the thought that she was dancing in her pointe shoes *onstage*. If only there was an audience instead of examiners and lovely famous choreography instead of class exercises, it would be just like being a real ballerina. Tash was nervous when the rises exercise at the *barre* started and she felt her ankles wobble a bit the first time she went *en pointe*. She gritted her teeth and tried to carry on smiling, and after a few more rises, she felt better and stronger.

But she was still nervous when they came to the *arabesque* exercise. She could feel the tension from her friends all around her, too – this was the one everyone was dreading the most. Tash had been able to do the exercise well in the last few classes, but she knew that Anisha still hadn't really got the hang of it. She looked worriedly across at Anisha, who was standing opposite her on the other side of the *barre*. Anisha looked terrified. Tash gave her a weak smile, but she didn't feel very confident herself. Balancing in an *arabesque* in the studio was one thing; it was different onstage. The floor wasn't the same as the studio floor she was used to dancing on, and Tash couldn't stop thinking about the teachers, watching every tiny movement she made.

The music started and Tash stepped neatly up onto her right foot, pointing her left foot out behind her in a low *arabesque*. She made sure that she was only holding on to the *barre* with her fingertips so that it would be easier to let go. She looked up, straight ahead of her, and raised her arms gently up and away from the *barre*, holding them out to first *arabesque*. One second…two…she was balancing, she really was! She tried to focus only on her own dancing, but she had seen Anisha struggling to let go of the *barre* and now she saw her friend wobble and come down too early. Tash bit her lip to stop herself gasping out loud. Luckily Anisha managed to keep smiling and to land neatly enough, but Tash's heart plummeted for her. She knew that Anisha would be upset that she'd messed up so obviously.

Next they had to repeat the exercise on the other leg: the foot that Tash had injured. She was nervous and her foot wobbled a bit as she stepped up onto it. Tash gritted her teeth, gripped the *barre* and tried to hold her foot steady. When the right point in the music came, she lifted her hands gently off the *barre* – and balanced! She'd been worried, but she'd managed to get her body to do what it was supposed to, and now the feeling of balancing onstage in an *arabesque* was more amazing than anything she'd felt before.

This time, even Anisha managed to balance, and Tash exchanged a happy smile with her. Even though there had been lots of times when she'd wished she could be having fun with her friends, all those lunchtime physio sessions had been worth it because they'd made her feet strong enough to do this. She'd managed to help Anisha get through the exam preparation, too, and now they were both balancing beautifully together. The hardest part of the exam was over, and they had nearly finished.

The *courus* exercise in the centre hurt just as much as it did in the studio, but as she moved across the floor in time with her friends, Tash tried to think about the fact that she had a whole stage to dance on, with wings and curtains and stage lights, and just before the music ended, there was a tiny moment where she forgot this was an exam and she felt like she was just dancing because it was what she loved to do.

"Thank you, girls," said Mr Watkins, when they'd finished. "You can go now."

There was no chance of anyone doing any work in English that morning, and Mr Kent knew it. The boys in the school had their ballet exams the next day and all they were interested in was finding out from the girls what their exam had been like; the girls slumped down into their seats as soon as they got to the classroom, the adrenaline and nerves turning into exhaustion.

"Anyone feel like turning the experience of doing a ballet exam into a short story?" Mr Kent asked hopefully, though Tash could tell he knew it was a long shot. "No? Okay then, you can talk quietly if you must, or get your books out and do a bit of reading." Most people got a book out, but no one opened one. There was too much to talk about and too much to think about. Tash knew even if she opened her book where she'd left off, she wouldn't understand a single word on the page.

"That wasn't too bad," sighed Dani. "I only forgot the steps in one exercise, and I copied you, Tash, so maybe they didn't notice."

"Even if they did, they won't expect us to be perfect at every single thing, will they?" Tash asked. Nobody knew. They all looked at each other in silence for a moment, and Tash guessed that everyone was thinking about the small mistakes they'd made. Tash felt *pretty* sure that a few small mistakes wouldn't mean they'd failed the exam, but she couldn't be *sure* sure.

"Three whole days to wait for the results!" groaned Toril.

"I'm going to spend the entire time wishing I'd landed better in the jumps," said Laura.

"I wish I hadn't messed up that *arabesque*,"

sighed Anisha. "But there's nothing we can do now."

"Yes there is," said Tash. Everyone looked at her curiously. She put her hand up to get Mr Kent's attention. "Can we go to the computer room?" she asked, when he looked over at her. "We need to make a programme for our dance-club performance."

Mr Kent agreed, and the girls made their way to the computer room.

"How do you feel?" Tash asked Anisha.

"Okay," Anisha replied uncertainly. "I don't think I did too badly, apart from falling out of the *arabesque*. I'm just worried that it's too late and that they made their decision about me while I was getting bored and staring into space."

Tash wished she could say something to make Anisha stop worrying, but she knew saying it would all be fine would be meaningless. All she could do was try to make Anisha think about other things. She linked her arm through Anisha's and gave her an affectionate squeeze, and then linked arms with Dani on the other side. They'd find out soon enough if Anisha would be staying with her friends, and until then, they had a dance-club performance to work on!

Chapter 12

At lunchtime, everyone who was in dance club went outside to practise for their performance. It had rained all weekend, but now the sun was shining and everything was bright green and full of spring freshness. Tash breathed in the refreshing air and spread her arms out to soak up as much sun as she could. It was only the end of March, so it wasn't really hot yet, but after days of being stuck inside staring out at grey skies, it felt amazing to be outside and not getting rained on.

The grass had dried during the morning so they could dance properly without worrying about getting muddy in all the sections of the street dance that were on the floor. Laughter rang out across the school field as they danced. The girls were suddenly hyped up on adrenaline left over from their exam, and the promise of the Easter holidays just around the corner, and the boys were full of jumpy nerves about their own exam, and when they'd gone through all of the dances properly once, everything started to get silly.

Tash toppled over and knocked Anisha off-balance when they were running through the contemporary dance for a second time. "Sorry, sorry!" she cried, holding her hand out to help Anisha up.

"So am I," said Anisha, taking Tash's hand and looking up at her from the ground.

"What for?" Tash asked.

"This," Anisha replied with a cheeky grin, and she yanked hard on Tash's hand, pulling her down to the grass beside her.

Dani giggled, and Tash couldn't help laughing too as she fell forwards. She looked around at the others. Some of the boys were chasing each other in a circle around the rest of the group, a few people were marking through the street-dance steps with Jonah, and others were practising the tap dance. The end of term was approaching fast, and Tash was excited about seeing Mum and going home for the Easter holidays. But she didn't want the days to whizz by like she had at the start of term. No way. She loved being at school with her friends. Plus, the dance-club performance was on Thursday evening, after the last full day of term, and what they needed was for time to slow down!

"I wish we had a bit more time to perfect the dances for the performance," said Dani. "We only have one more rehearsal in the studio left!"

Tash felt a shiver of anticipation run through

her at the thought. "I can't wait to get back on that stage," she said, imagining herself back where she'd danced in the exam that morning.

"And *this* time," said Anisha, "it's not going to be a horrible exam. It's going to be *fun!*"

"I know you're all worrying about the exam results later today," Miss Anderbel said at the beginning of their Thursday-morning ballet class. Tash flashed an anxious look at Anisha, who was staring intently at their teacher. For a moment, Tash was terrified that Miss Anderbel was going to give the results out right then. She didn't think that she wanted to be in a ballet class when she found out how she'd done. At the time, she'd thought it went well, but with every hour that had passed since, she'd become more and more unsure. What if she hadn't done well? If she had to do a ballet class right after finding out she'd failed, she knew she'd never be able to lift up her head and dance.

But Miss Anderbel had something entirely different in mind. "I'll be taking each of you out of form time this afternoon to talk about how you did. But now, I think we all need to get our minds off ballet for an hour or two," she continued. "You've got your dance-club performance this evening, haven't you? Mr Edwards and I thought you and the boys might want to use this morning's class to practise for that, so we're all going to go and use the stage. You should have at least *one* rehearsal onstage before you perform there!"

Tash was relieved, and she grinned at Dani as she grabbed her bottle of water and followed the rest of her class out of the studio to get their things and move to the stage.

Everyone ran to get their character shoes for the tap dance, and they practised that first. Tash could tell from the sounds all around her that everyone was dancing in time with each other at last and she grinned at Anisha, who gave her a big smile back. Then they did the street dance.

Amazing Arabesque

Tash and Anisha sat in the front row of the auditorium seats and watched their friends dancing on the stage. It looked even better than it had in the common room or the studio! The stage was quite small, so the dancers took up all the space and made it full of life. Bright lights shone down on them from above as they jumped and spun, and the music sounded louder than ever, filling the auditorium right to the back.

Finally, they worked on Dani's contemporary dance, doing it as well as they could without the Year Eights, who hadn't been let out of their morning class, even though it was the last one before the holidays. Tash was so glad Miss Anderbel was their teacher, and she really hoped they could impress her with their performance at the end of the day. Thinking about that reminded Tash that, by that point, they'd know whether they'd impressed her in the exam, too.

"Let's try it again from the beginning," said Dani, standing on the floor right in front of the stage and looking up at them. "Lily-May, make sure you bend your arm back like Tash does in the circle bit."

Tash didn't think Lily-May would much like being criticised by someone her own age, but surprisingly, Lily-May didn't seem to think anything of it. She nodded seriously at Dani and demonstrated what she was meant to do. "Yeah," said Dani. "That's good."

Tash smiled, watching her friend. Something about doing this on the Aurora House stage made it all seem real and professional, as if Dani was a grown-up choreographer preparing her dancers for an important performance. It made Tash want to try harder than ever. She wanted her teachers and the rest of the school to be entertained by and impressed with her dancing, but more than that, she wanted them to be amazed by the steps Dani had made up, and she wanted the same for Anisha's tap dance, too. Her best friends had helped to make her birthday special and to make

Aurora House feel like home; this was how Tash could make everyone see that Dani and Anisha were wonderful and talented. It was the best way she could thank them for being her friends.

That afternoon, Tash sat in her form room beside Anisha with Dani in front of her, turned around in her seat so that the three of them were facing each other. They watched their classmates go out of the room to meet with Miss Anderbel or Mr Edwards in the empty classrooms next door. One by one they left and came back smiling. Laura. Toril. Lily-May. Then it was Dani's turn. She came back with a huge smile on her face.

"Tag," she said, tapping Tash on the shoulder. "You're next." Tash gave Anisha's hand a quick squeeze under the desk and got up. She smoothed her school skirt down as she walked out of the room, feeling just as nervous as she had when she'd stepped onto the stage to begin the exam.

Tash pushed open the door to the music room,

where Miss Anderbel was waiting for her. The pass mark was sixty out of a hundred, she reminded herself. Anything higher than sixty was fine.

"Hi, Tash," said Miss Anderbel. "You have absolutely no need to look so worried."

Her smile was contagious and Tash couldn't help relaxing into a smile herself, before she'd even glanced at the report Miss Anderbel handed her. She looked down at the paper with the Aurora House logo at the top. Lines of neat writing danced in and out of focus, and then suddenly the mark jumped out at her. Eighty-nine. Eighty-nine! She laughed. She couldn't help it. When she looked back up, Miss Anderbel was still smiling at her.

"Well done," the teacher said. "There are always areas for improvement – I've written about that on your report. But if you come back after Easter and carry on dancing like you have this term, I'm sure you'll get better at those things too."

Amazing Arabesque

"I will," promised Tash. She couldn't believe she'd done so well. And that was while she'd been feeling anxious and homesick for the first half of term – how much better could she be now that she felt like the ballet studio *was* home? She couldn't wait to come back next term and find out.

"Thanks, Miss Anderbel," she said.

"Send Anisha in, will you?" Miss Anderbel asked. Tash nodded and the smile fell away from her face. Suddenly she was even more nervous about Anisha's results than she had been about her own. Talking to Miss Anderbel, she'd felt like this was the perfect end to the term, but now she remembered that there was still a chance for everything to go horribly wrong.

Tash smiled at her friends as she walked back into the form room.

"You did good?" Dani asked. Tash nodded quickly and turned her eyes to Anisha.

"Your turn," she said. Anisha bit her lip and stood up.

"Right," she said. "Here goes."

"Good luck," said Dani and Tash. Tash sat on Dani's desk and they watched their friend leave. They were both silent for a moment.

"So?" asked Dani, eventually.

"Eighty-nine," said Tash. Dani's eyebrows shot up.

"Wow!" she said. "I was pleased with seventy-five."

"That's brilliant," said Tash, thrilled that Dani had done so well.

"Eighty-nine, though!" said Dani. "That's like...amazing."

"Thanks," said Tash.

She looked down at the report, realizing that she hadn't actually read any of it yet. When she did, it was obvious that her teachers were pleased with her, and the things she needed to improve on were the small things that Miss Anderbel always pulled her up on in class. She could definitely work on them over the holidays and come back ready to wow her teachers even more. She folded the paper and slipped off the desk to put it in her homework diary.

Anisha was gone for ages and Tash was worried. It hadn't taken Miss Anderbel very long at all to tell her she'd done well. What if being gone a long time meant that Anisha was getting bad news?

At last the door opened and Anisha came back in. She looked quickly at Tash and Dani, then went to tell Donna that she was next. Tash and Dani didn't take their eyes off her; they were desperate to know that she was okay.

"We had a serious talk about motivation and stuff," Anisha said quietly, when she sat back down next to Tash. "I explained that I'd found it hard just repeating exercises over and over." She paused and Tash and Dani looked at her in suspense and dread in case the serious talk had ended with bad news. "Miss Anderbel said I need to find a way to cope with that because I'm going to have to do another six years of ballet exams at Aurora House alongside my friends. I got sixty-six!"

Dani whooped with joy and leaned across the desk to give Anisha a hug. Tash hugged her too, feeling relieved and happier than she'd felt all term, not caring that the rest of the class was looking at them. Anisha was staying in their class! Her lovely ballet family would still be here to get each other through another term, and then another year, and all the years of school after that. Maybe, if they were really lucky, one day they'd all be part of the City Ballet family, just like the dancers they'd met at the beginning of term.

The dance-club performance was after their contemporary dance class. Miss Carter allowed them to finish class half an hour early so that they could go to the stage and get ready. While Dani and Anisha put the programmes out on the seats, Tash walked onto the stage and tried a few movements from the contemporary dance. She loved the feeling of being onstage – looking up and seeing bright lights above you and catching sight of your friends in the wings. And this wasn't just any stage. This was the Aurora House stage. She remembered coming to look at the school before her audition to get in and hoping that one day she'd get to dance here, and she'd been so disappointed when she had to miss out on the Christmas performance. Now it was finally her turn.

People started to file in and take their seats as other dance classes and academic lessons finished, so Tash and the others scurried away to put on their character shoes. They didn't have costumes, so they were dressed in comfortable dance clothes like leggings and T-shirts: not a single leotard or bun in sight. When the auditorium was full, Dani turned the lights down so that only the stage was lit up. Tash walked out onto the stage as they'd planned. She had to talk to the whole school! It was much scarier than she'd thought it would be.

"Hi, everyone," she began.

"Louder!" she heard Anisha whisper from the wings.

"We're the Year Seven and Eight dance club," Tash continued, raising her voice so that it carried clearly all the way to the back of the small theatre. "We started making up dances together in half-term, just for fun. But then school started again and we realized that, with ballet exams coming up, *fun* was exactly what we all needed." A laugh sounded across the audience like a wave and a few people cheered. Tash grinned. "So we carried on dancing, with one rule only: no ballet allowed. And here's what we did. We hope you enjoy it."

The audience clapped and Tash hurried off the stage. As soon as she got into the wings, Anisha grabbed her into a hug.

"That was perfect!" Anisha said.

"So scary!" laughed Tash, her teeth chattering

together with nerves and excitement. But there was no time for more talking. Jonah walked onto the stage, followed by Dani and the others who were doing the street dance.

"This street dance was choreographed by Jonah Elliott," said Donna, stepping forwards to speak to the audience, and then darting back to her place.

Tash was in charge of the music for this one, so she pressed play and then hurried back to the front of the wings with Anisha to watch. It was great: everyone was perfectly in time and Jonah and some of the others had little solos in the middle which made everyone in the audience cheer. Tash could tell that the audience were enjoying it as much as the dancers. She nodded along to the music, watching Dani crouching, jumping, spinning, kicking, and doing everything in the most un-ballet way imaginable. Everyone onstage was smiling and, though the auditorium was too dark for the dancers to see the audience's faces, Tash hoped the rest of the school was smiling too.

They ran off the stage into the wings while the audience applauded at the end, and Tash high-fived Dani as she passed. Her contemporary piece was next, so Tash and Anisha and the other eight dancers, a mix of girls and boys from their year and Year Eight, ran lightly onto the stage.

"This dance was choreographed by Dani Taylor," said Tash.

The music began and Tash started to dance, feeling nervous because she so wanted it to be good. She flowed through the steps, turning and stretching, and her nerves floated up and away into the bright lights shining down on her. It felt like the most special performance she'd ever done, because she knew the steps had been created by Dani, and the whole dance-club idea had been thought of to help Anisha. She was dancing on the Aurora House stage and she didn't feel like the girl who had come here to look around the school and try out for a place any more; she felt that she belonged here, a part of the school. She passed Anisha on the stage as they twirled around each other in the middle of the dance, and they shared a smile. There was nowhere on earth that Tash would rather be than dancing onstage at her school, surrounded by friends.

The audience clapped and clapped at the end, and Tash made Dani come out and take a bow by herself because she hadn't been in the dance. Tash clapped harder than anyone, and as she watched Dani turning bright red and smiling in the middle of the stage, she caught sight of Miss Anderbel and Mr Watkins in the front row with their heads close together, nodding and talking and looking at Dani. Tash was *so* pleased they'd seen what her friend could do.

"And finally, a dance choreographed by the wonderful Anisha Acharya!" said Dani, just before the tap dance began.

They'd definitely saved the most fun for last.

Ballet Stars

The audience tapped their feet in time with the music – they were an audience full of dancers, after all, and most of them couldn't resist. Tash bet that lots of them wished they could get up and join in, and that thought only made her enjoy it even more. She was making people want to dance!

Hopping and tapping and swinging her arms in time with her best friends, Tash wanted to do this for ever. She caught Anisha's eye and could tell that she did, too. The dance got faster and faster, building to a fantastic rhythm with everyone dancing in three lines, perfectly in time with each other and smiling so much that it hurt. They tapped forwards to the front of the stage and moved into one long line, doing time steps all together, and then on the very last note of the music, they stamped one foot down and threw one arm up into the air, looking up high into the rows of lights above the stage.

The audience burst into wild applause, clapping

and cheering, and Tash and the others bowed again and again, smiling at each other with delight. Dance club was a total success! They bowed one final time and filed off the stage and into the wings. Someone turned the auditorium lights back on and they could hear the rest of the school leaving.

Tash took her character shoes off slowly. She didn't want the performance to be over already. Everyone was talking excitedly and they gathered up dance shoes and bottles of water from the wings and began to leave. Tash wandered back onto the stage in bare feet, holding her shoes in one hand. Dani and Anisha followed her. Almost all of the audience had gone now, apart from Mr Watkins and Miss Anderbel.

"Well done," said Mr Watkins. "You all obviously put a great deal of effort into that performance."

"Thanks," Tash, Dani and Anisha replied in unison.

"I was particularly impressed with the choreography you two did, and Jonah's too," said Mr Watkins. "You've all got bright futures ahead of you."

Anisha and Dani grinned at each other.

"And, Tash, I'm amazed at the difference I've seen in you this term," continued the head teacher. "You have so much more confidence in your dancing."

"And a great sense of fun," added Miss Anderbel. "You made me want to put a pair of tap shoes on!"

They all laughed, and the teachers walked off.

"That was so much fun," said Anisha, sitting down on the edge of the stage with her legs dangling down towards the floor.

"The best thing we've done all term," agreed Tash sitting down next to her. Dani sat on her other side.

"Thank you for coming up with the idea," Anisha said to Tash and Dani.

Amazing Arabesque

Tash smiled and put an arm around each of her two best friends. "I wish we could do it all over again right now."

"Me too," said Dani. "I love ballet classes, but nothing is as good as dancing onstage."

"Nothing in the whole world," agreed Anisha.

With all the worry of the exam results and all the excitement of the performance, Tash had very nearly forgotten that Mum was taking her and her friends out for a special birthday surprise on Friday afternoon. Mum had told Tash that she'd agreed with Dani's and Anisha's parents that they'd come to pick their children up from Aurora House at six o'clock instead of at lunchtime, which was the time that school officially finished, but she still wouldn't give anything else away.

After breakfast, they all packed up the clothes and things they wanted to take home for the holidays and then they hung out in Coppélia, chatting and listening to music and telling each other their plans for the holidays. Toril had left already to go back to Norway, travelling to the airport earlier that morning. Laura and Donna were still packing when the door opened and Mum poked her head around.

"Mum!" cried Tash, and flew into her arms.

After a long hug and lots of kisses, Mum untangled herself and reached into her bag.

"Happy birthday," she said, holding out an envelope.

Tash opened it and pulled out four tickets to see City Ballet performing *Romeo and Juliet*. She screamed and threw her arms around Mum again. Dani and Anisha came over to see what the surprise was and read the tickets that were still in Tash's hand. Then they were squealing with delight too.

The curtain rose in the dark auditorium and Tash relaxed into her seat. She'd seen bits of *Romeo and Juliet* before, and she knew the story because she'd seen the film. But she'd never seen the whole ballet before. It took her breath away. The costumes and sets were grand and beautiful – long dresses in rich reds and greens, an elaborate ballroom and a pretty balcony draped in flowers and vines.

The dancing was like no ballet she'd ever seen. It was classical ballet, but it was *nothing* like what they did in class. It was so emotional, there was storytelling in every step, and she really believed that the dancers *were* the characters. They looked like they were being swept along by the music, just as Romeo and Juliet were swept along by fate, and it didn't look like choreography at all; the dancers made the steps look as if they were just *happening*.

"This is what it's all for," said Anisha, her voice full of awe, when the curtain came down and the lights came up for the interval.

Sitting next to her, Tash nodded silently, her mind still with the dancers on the stage.

"*This*," Anisha repeated. "This is what I want to do."

"Me too," said Dani, and when Tash turned to look at her, her friend's eyes were shining. "I'm going to work harder than anyone else has ever worked, *ever*, if it means I'll be able to do that one day."

"Let's promise," said Tash. "One day, that will be us. And we'll do *anything* to help each other get there."

She took one of Anisha's hands and one of Dani's, and they held hands with each other too.

"Promise," said Dani.

"Promise," said Anisha.

Tash looked at them both. It wouldn't be easy and she knew there'd be some things they couldn't help each other with, but there were lots of things they could: getting through a whole term away from home, keeping up with schoolwork, carrying on dancing when you were having a bad day.

"Promise," said Tash.

They all smiled, filled with a secret power. They would keep each other happy. And whenever their dream started to slip away from one of them, the other two would grab it back and keep it going until they were all holding on again. Tash looked down towards the stage and imagined herself, Dani and Anisha, three best friends, dancing there all together.

Basic Ballet Positions

All of the wondeful ballet moves Tash, Dani and Anisha learn begin and end in one of these five basic positions...

First position
The feet point in opposite directions, with heels touching. Arms are rounded to the front.

Second position
The feet point in opposite directions, with heels spaced approximately thirty centimetres apart. Arms are out to the sides, angled down and forward.

Third position

One foot is placed in front of the other so that the heel of the front foot is near the arch of the back foot. One arm is in first position, the other is in second position.

Fourth position

One foot is placed approximately thirty centimetres in front of the other. One arm is rounded and raised above the head, the other is in second position.

Fifth position

One foot is placed in front of the other, with the heel of one foot in contact with the toe of the other foot. Both arms are rounded and raised above the head.

Ballet Glossary

adage The name for the slow steps in the centre of the room, away from the barre.

arabesque A beautiful balance on one leg.

assemblé A jump where the feet come together at the end.

attitude A pose standing on one leg, the other leg raised with the knee bent.

battement glisse A faster version of *battement tendu*, with the foot lifted off the floor.

battement tendu A foot exercise where you stretch one leg out along the floor, keeping it straight all the way to the point of the foot.

chassé A soft smooth slide of the feet.

demi-pointe Dancing with the weight of the body on the toes and the ball of the foot.

développé A lifting and unfolding of one leg into the air, while balancing on the other.

en pointe Dancing on the very tips of the toes.

entrechat A jump directly upward, while crossing the feet before and behind several times in the air.

grand battement A high kick, keeping the supporting leg straight.

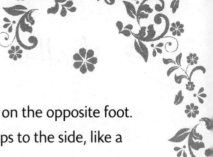

jeté A spring where you land on the opposite foot.

pas de bourrée Tiny little steps to the side, like a mouse.

pas de chat A cat hop from one foot to the other.

plié The first step practised in each class. You have to bend your knees slowly and make sure your feet are turned right out, with your heels firmly planted on the floor for as long as possible.

port de bras Arm movements.

révérence The curtsey at the end of class.

rond de jambe This is where you make a circle with your leg.

sissonne en arrière A jump from two feet onto one foot moving backwards.

sissonne en avant A jump from two feet onto one foot moving forwards.

soubresaut A jump off two feet, pointing your feet hard in the air.

turnout You have to stand with your legs and feet and hips all opened out and pointing to the side, not the front. This is the most important thing in ballet that everyone learns right from the start.

❋ Usborne Quicklinks ❋

For links to websites where you can watch
videos of ballet dancers, see excerpts of ballet
performances and find out more about ballet,
go to the Usborne Quicklinks Website at
www.usborne-quicklinks.com and enter
the keywords "ballet stars".

*When using the Internet, make sure you follow the Internet safety
guidelines displayed on the Usborne Quicklinks Website. Usborne
Publishing is not responsible for the content on any website other
than its own. We recommend that children are supervised while
on the Internet, that they do not use Internet chat rooms, and that
you use Internet filtering software to block unsuitable material.
For more information, see the "Net Help" area on the Usborne
Quicklinks Website.*

*Usborne Publishing is not responsible and does not accept liability
for the availability or content of any website other than its own,
or for any exposure to harmful, offensive, or inaccurate material
which may appear on the Web. Usborne Publishing will have no
liability for any damage or loss caused by viruses that may be
downloaded as a result of browsing the sites it recommends.*

Follow all of Tash's
Ballet Star dreams
in two other
sparkling stories...

❋ Perfect Pirouette ❋

It's Tash's first term at Aurora House, and she's thrilled
to be living with other girls who love ballet just as much
as she does! But when she starts to worry that her
dancing isn't as good as her new friends', Tash decides
to take a big risk. Will her plan lead to a perfect
pirouette...or a dancing disaster?

ISBN 9781409583530

❋ Sparkling Solo ❋

It's the summer term at Aurora House and Tash is so
excited about the end-of-year performance! She can't
wait to dance on a real stage for the first time, and
she's desperate to win the solo role of her dreams: the
Lilac Fairy. But Dani is struggling with stage fright. Can
Tash help her to sparkle in the spotlight?

ISBN 9781409583554

Also by Jane Lawes

Gym Stars

Summertime and Somersaults

Tara loves gym and spends all her time practising in her garden. When she joins Silverdale Gym Club she's catapulted into their star squad. But there's so much to learn. How will she ever catch up with her talented teammates?

ISBN: 9781409531791

ISBN: 9781409531807

Friendships and Backflips

Tara's training for her first ever competition and she's desperate to win a gold medal. But she's so busy learning the tricky routine that her best friends think she's deserted them. Can she find room in her life for her friends *and* gym?

ISBN: 9781409531814

Handsprings and Homework

Tara's through to a national competition, but she's training so hard that her homework is starting to pile up and she's in big trouble with her teachers. Can Tara finish all her work on time *and* win a gold medal?

For more *dazzling* reads
head to
www.usborne.com/fiction